For Lauren, my Fitz — H.F.
To my Buddy — J.S.

*A Note about Starfish*
Starfish live in the water. If you find a living one on the beach,
place it gently back in the water (using clean hands).
Never take a starfish out of the water.

Henry Holt and Company, *Publishers since 1866*
Henry Holt® is a registered trademark of Macmillan Publishing Group, LLC
120 Broadway, New York, NY 10271  •  mackids.com

Library of Congress Cataloging-in-Publication Data is available.
ISBN 978-1-250-23944-0

Our books may be purchased in bulk for promotional, educational, or
business use. Please contact your local bookseller or the Macmillan
Corporate and Premium Sales Department at (800) 221-7945 ext. 5442
or by email at MacmillanSpecialMarkets@macmillan.com.

First edition, 2021
Printed in China by Toppan Leefung Printing Ltd., Dongguang City,
Guangdong Province.

1  3  5  7  9  10  8  6  4  2

A Fitz and Cleo Book

# Fitz
## AND
# Cleo

Jonathan Stutzman & Heather Fox

Henry Holt and Company
New York

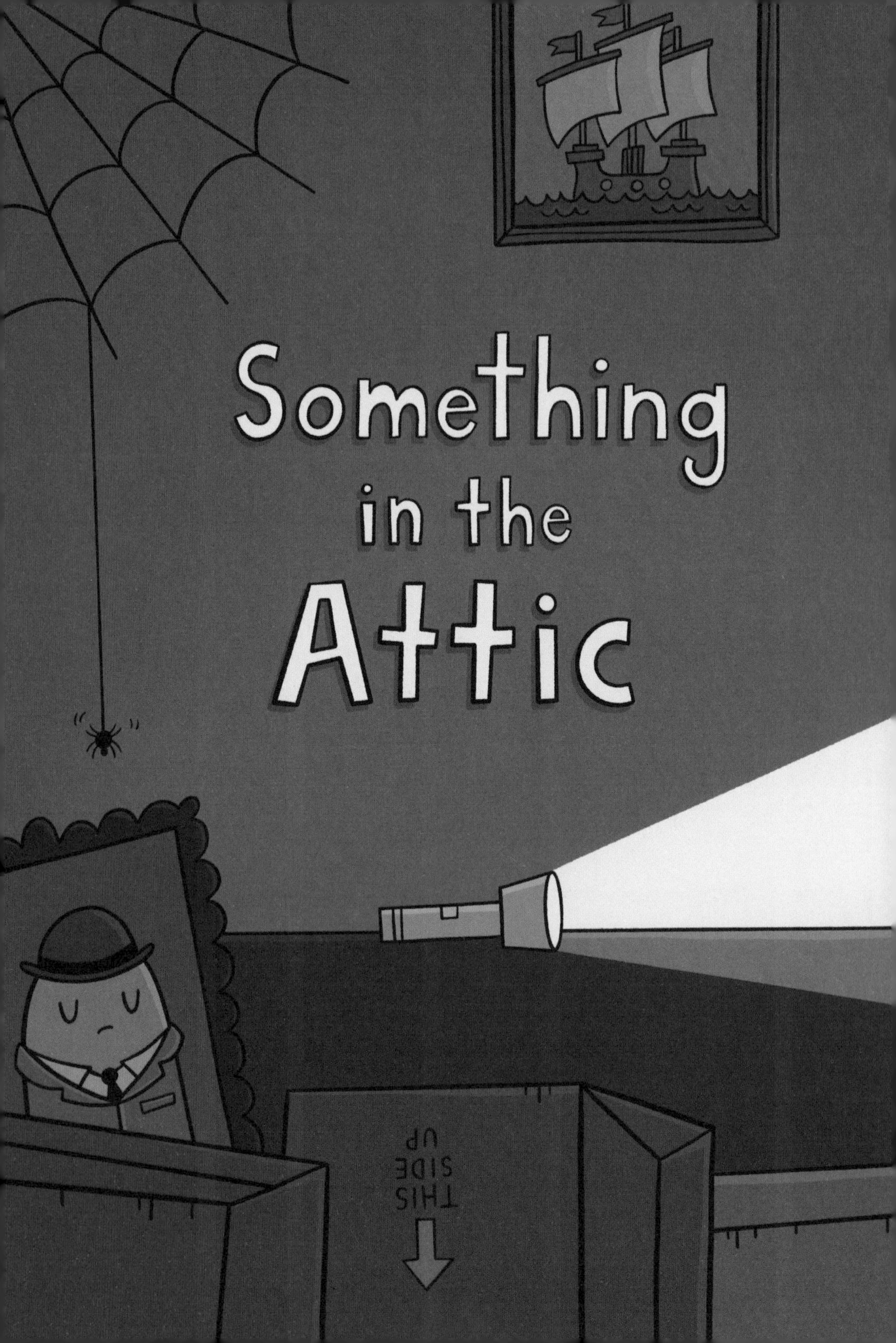
Something in the Attic
THIS SIDE UP

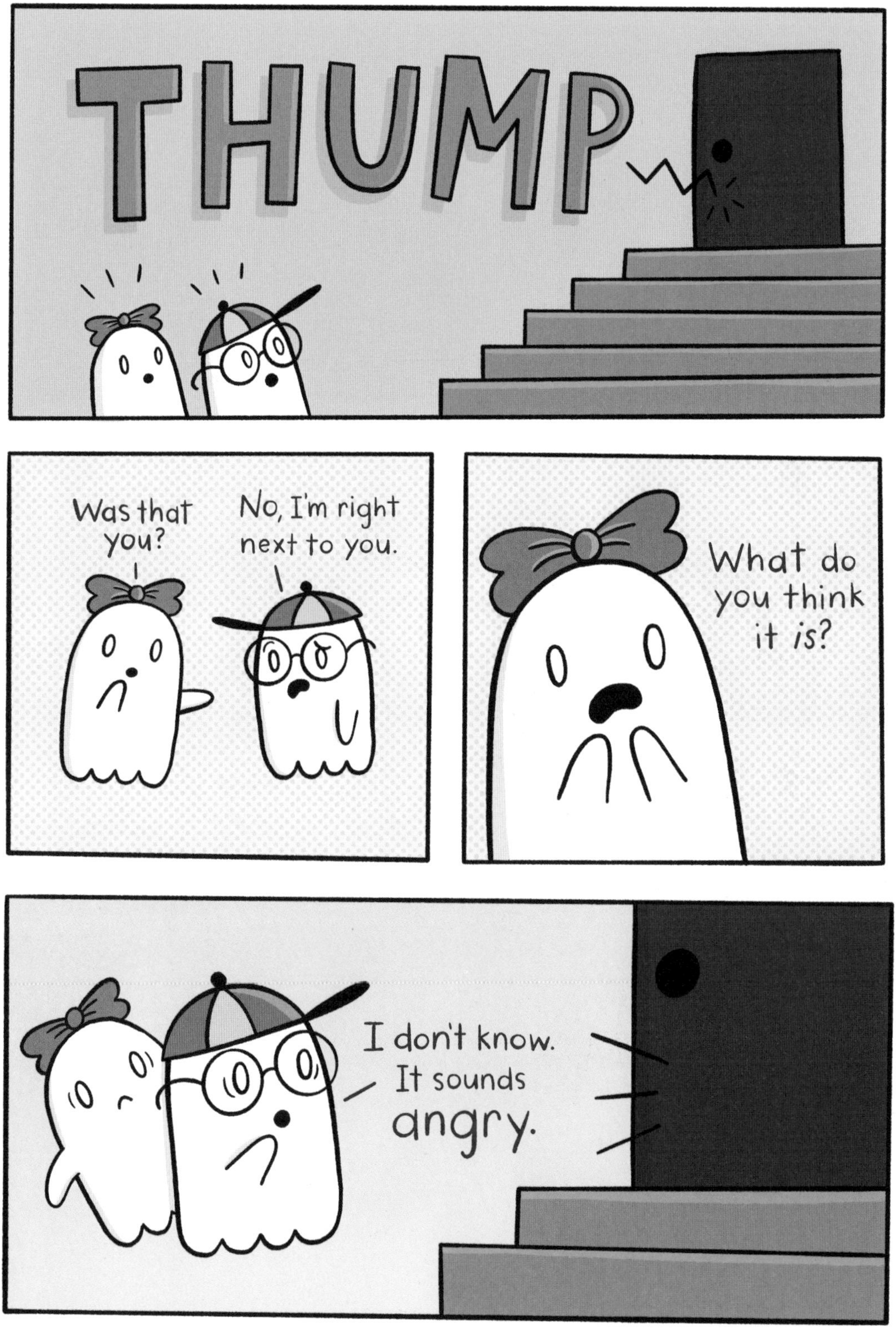
THUMP
Was that you?
No, I'm right next to you.
What do you think it *is*?
I don't know. It sounds angry.

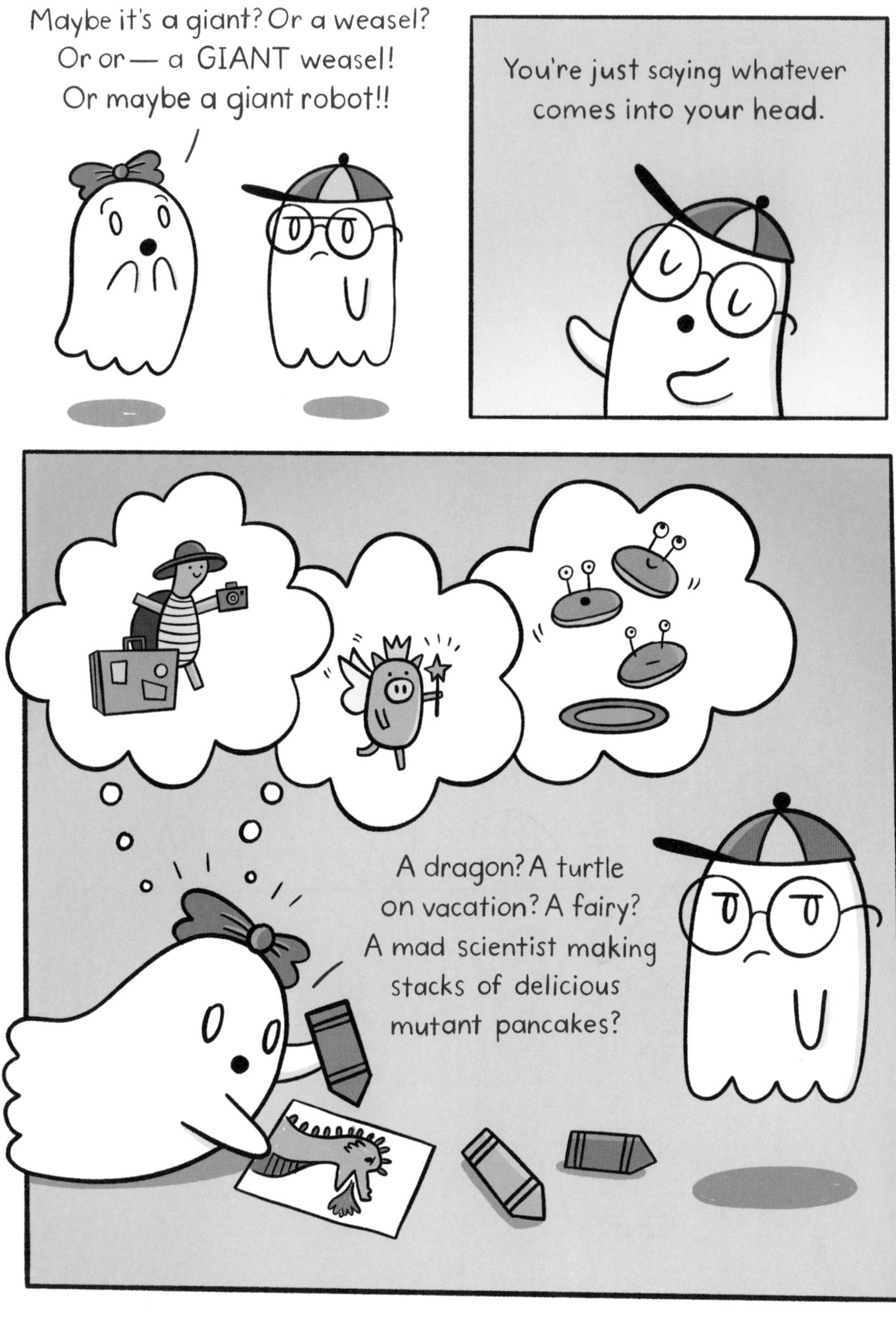
Maybe it's a giant? Or a weasel? Or or— a GIANT weasel! Or maybe a giant robot!!
You're just saying whatever comes into your head.
A dragon? A turtle on vacation? A fairy? A mad scientist making stacks of delicious mutant pancakes?

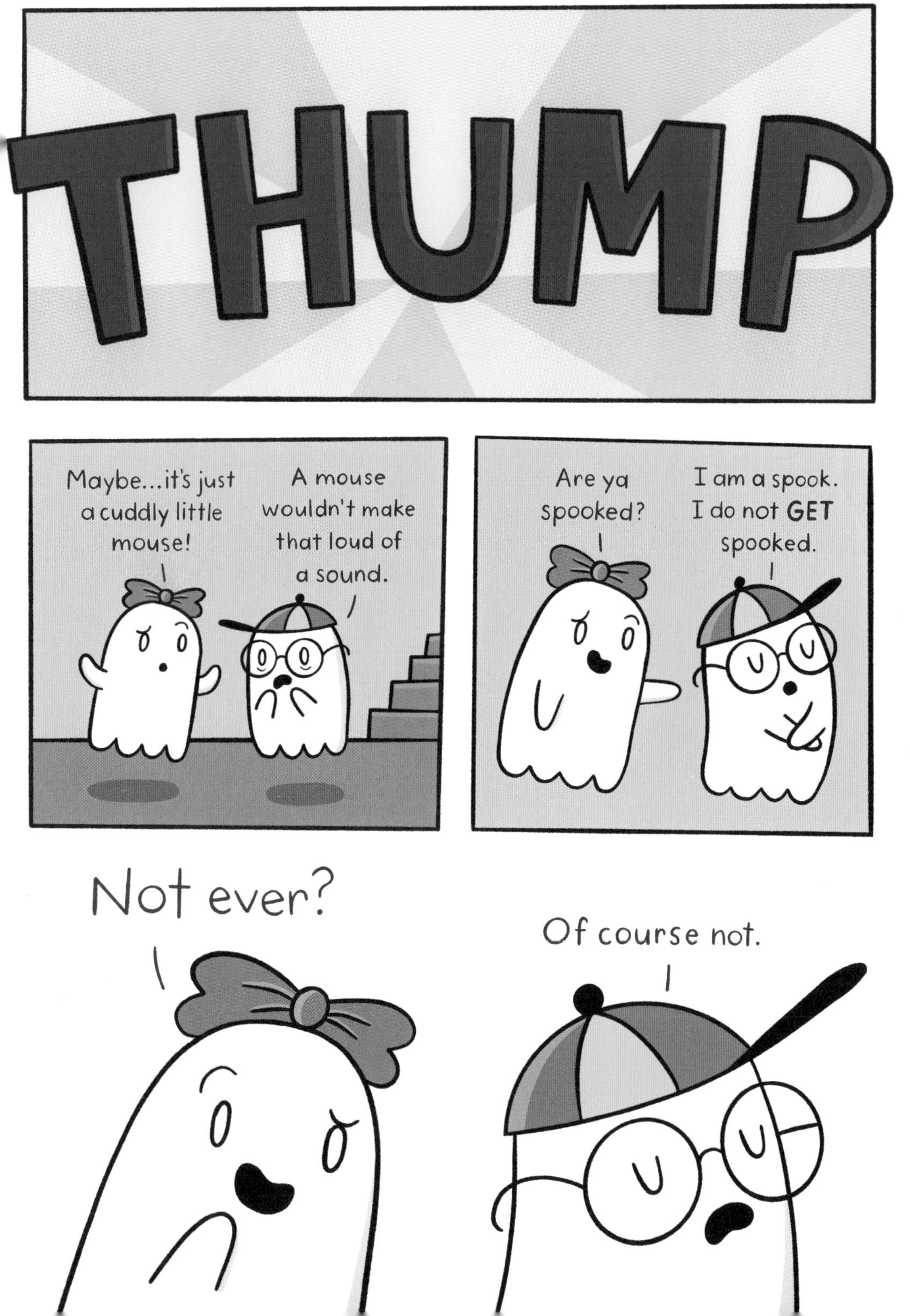
THUMP
Maybe...it's just a cuddly little mouse!
A mouse wouldn't make that loud of a sound.
Are ya spooked?
I am a spook. I do not GET spooked.
Not ever?
Of course not.

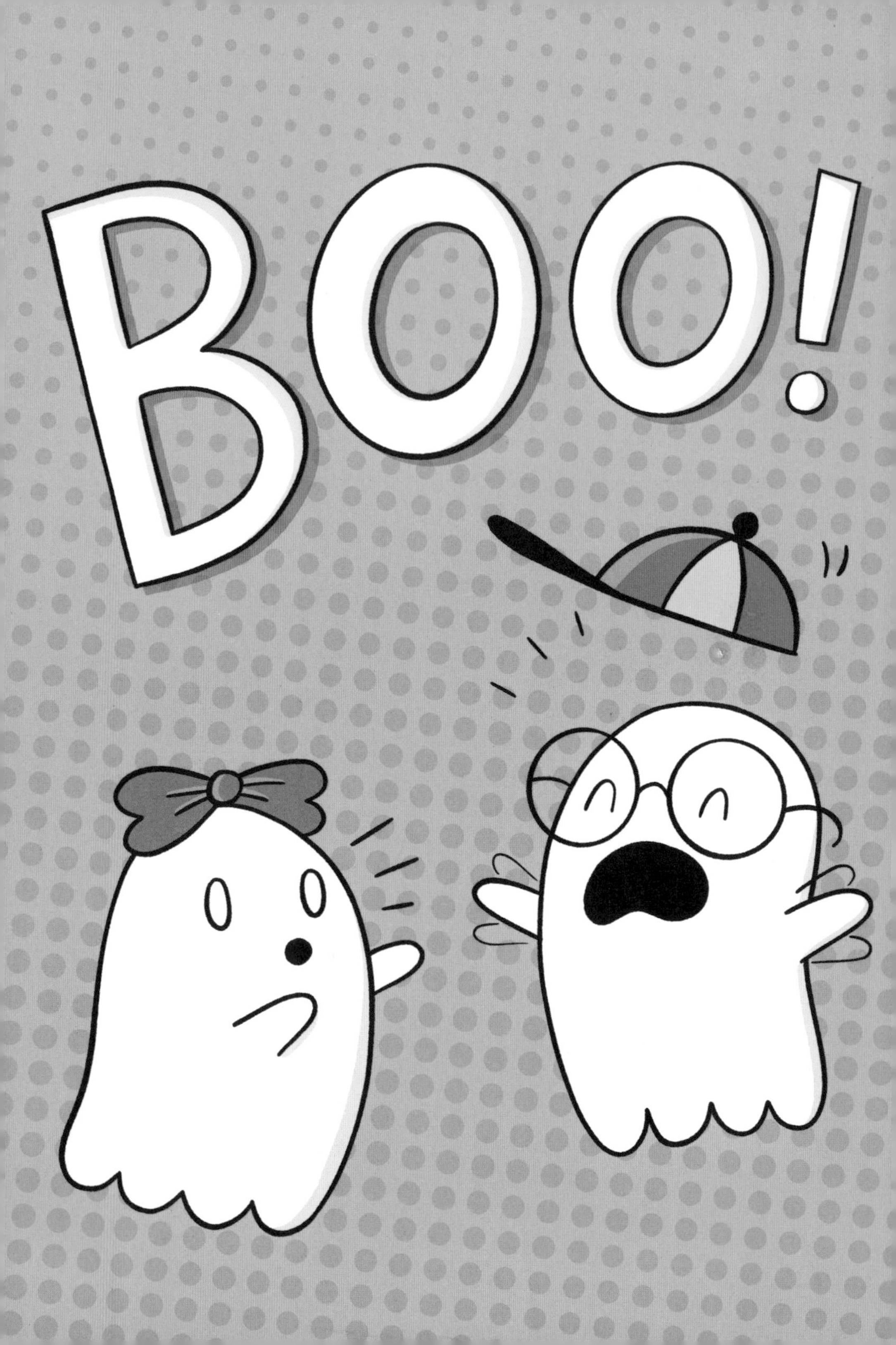
BOO!

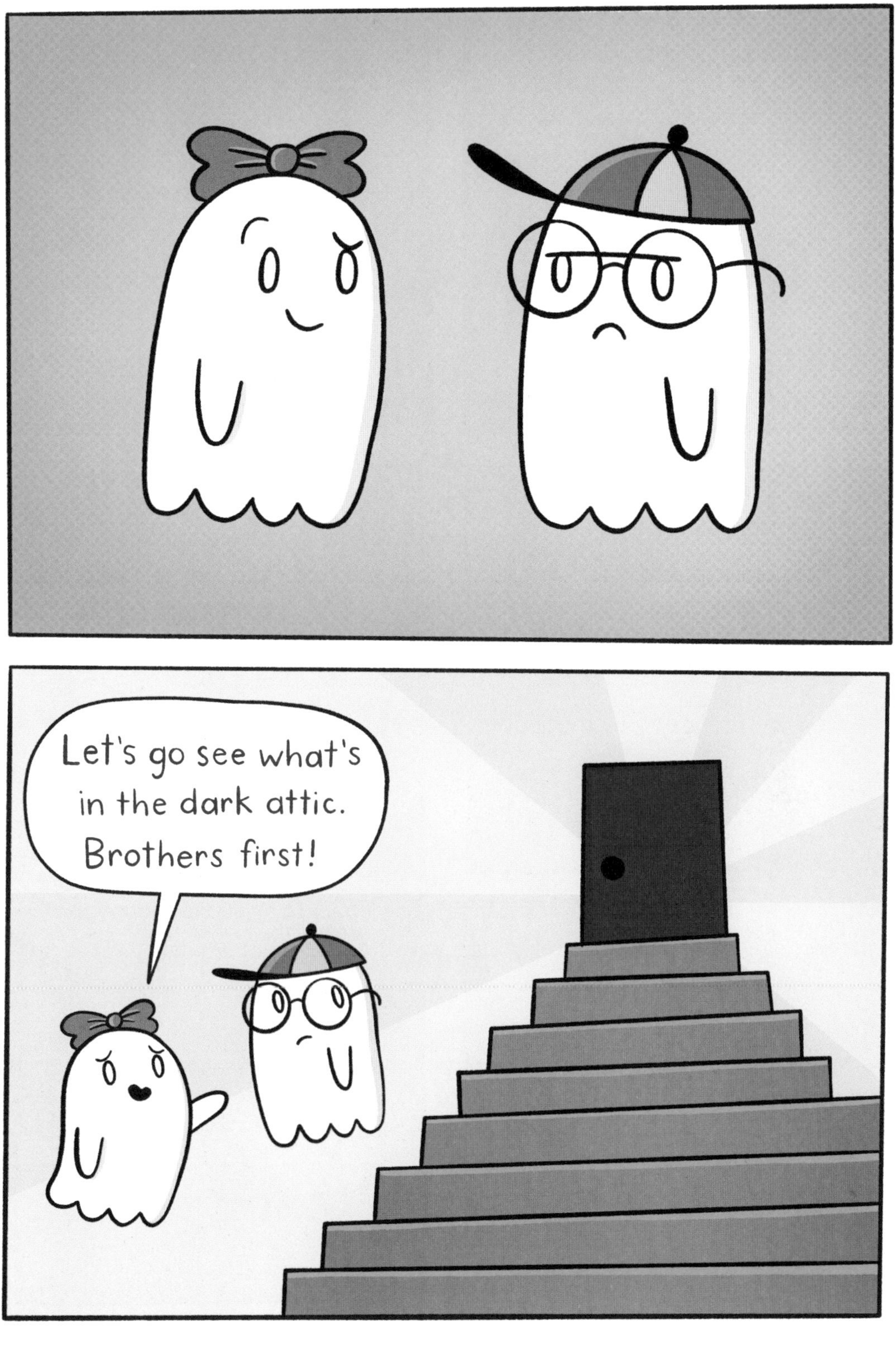
Let's go see what's in the dark attic. Brothers first!

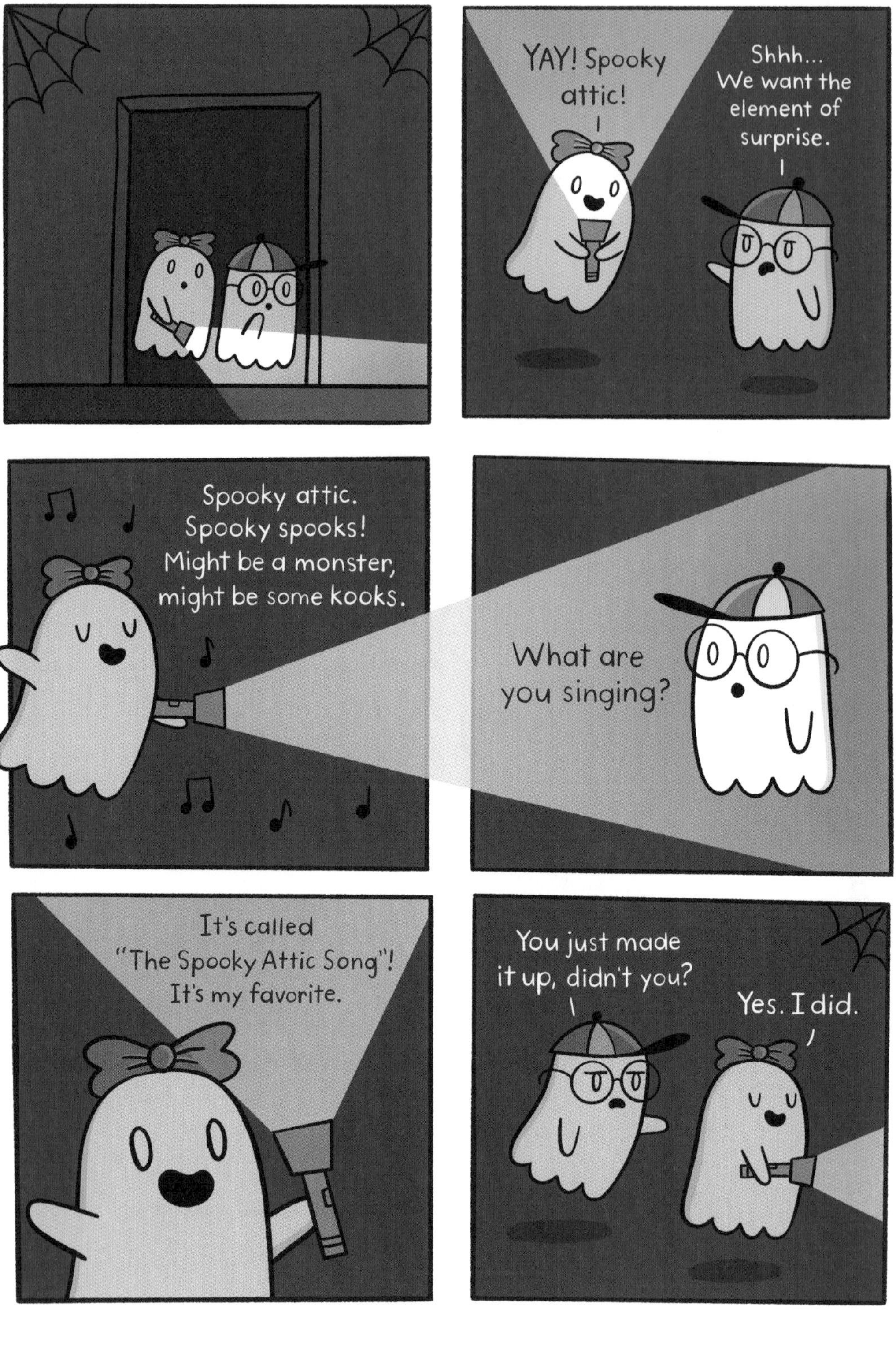
YAY! Spooky attic!
Shhh... We want the element of surprise.
Spooky attic. Spooky spooks! Might be a monster, might be some kooks.
What are you singing?
It's called "The Spooky Attic Song"! It's my favorite.
You just made it up, didn't you?
Yes. I did.

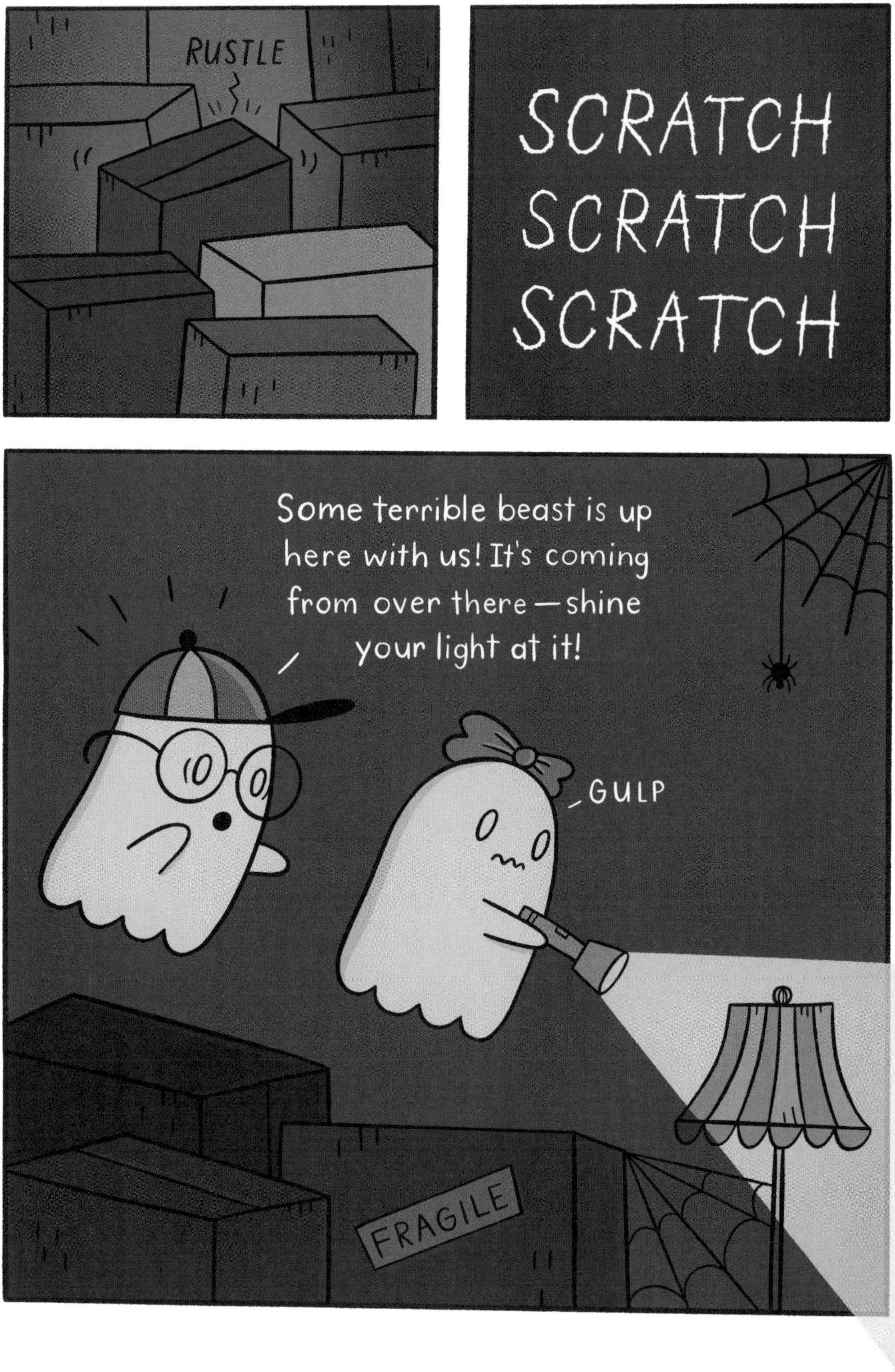
RUSTLE
SCRATCH
SCRATCH
SCRATCH
Some terrible beast is up here with us! It's coming from over there—shine your light at it!
GULP
FRAGILE

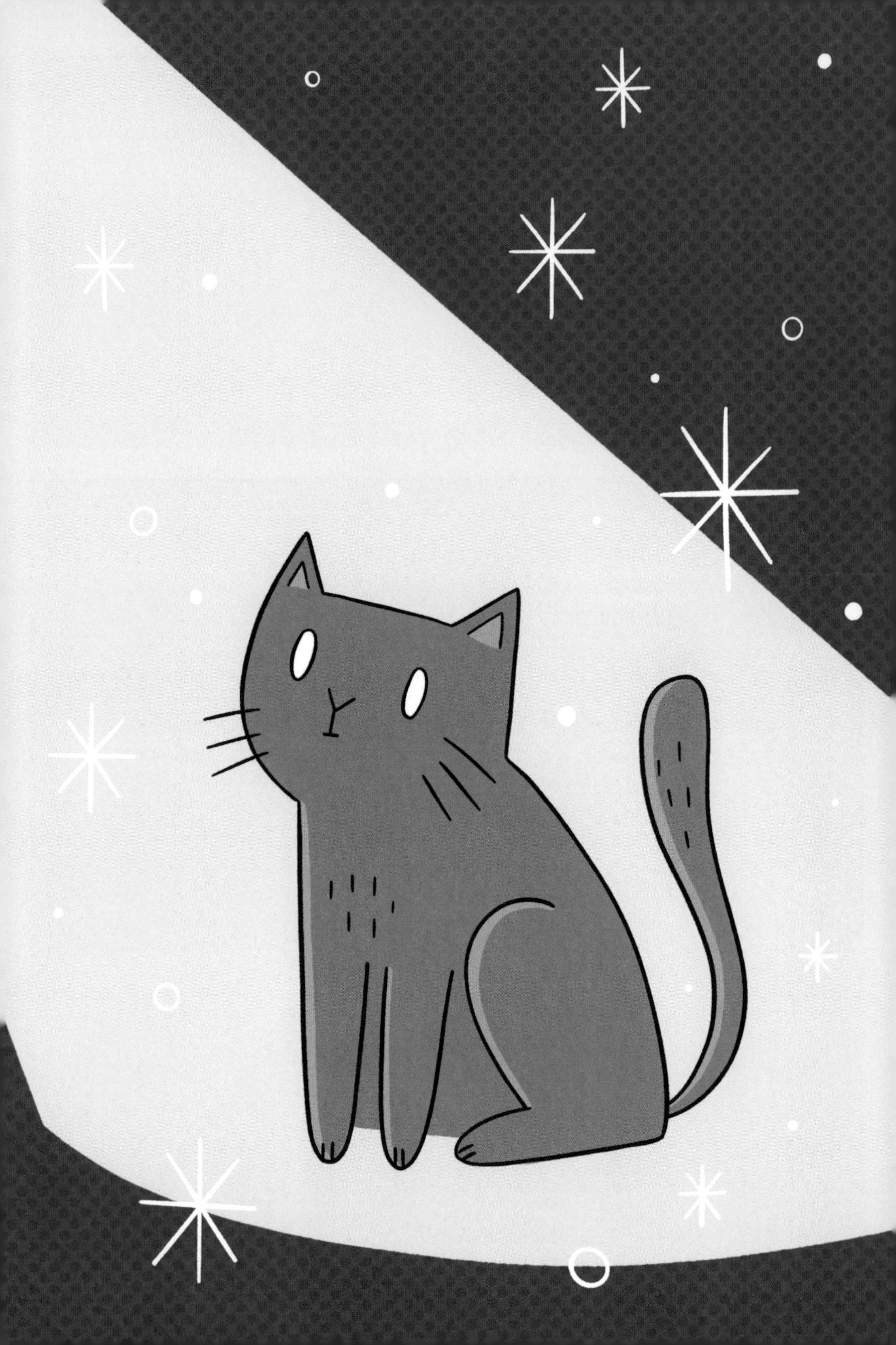

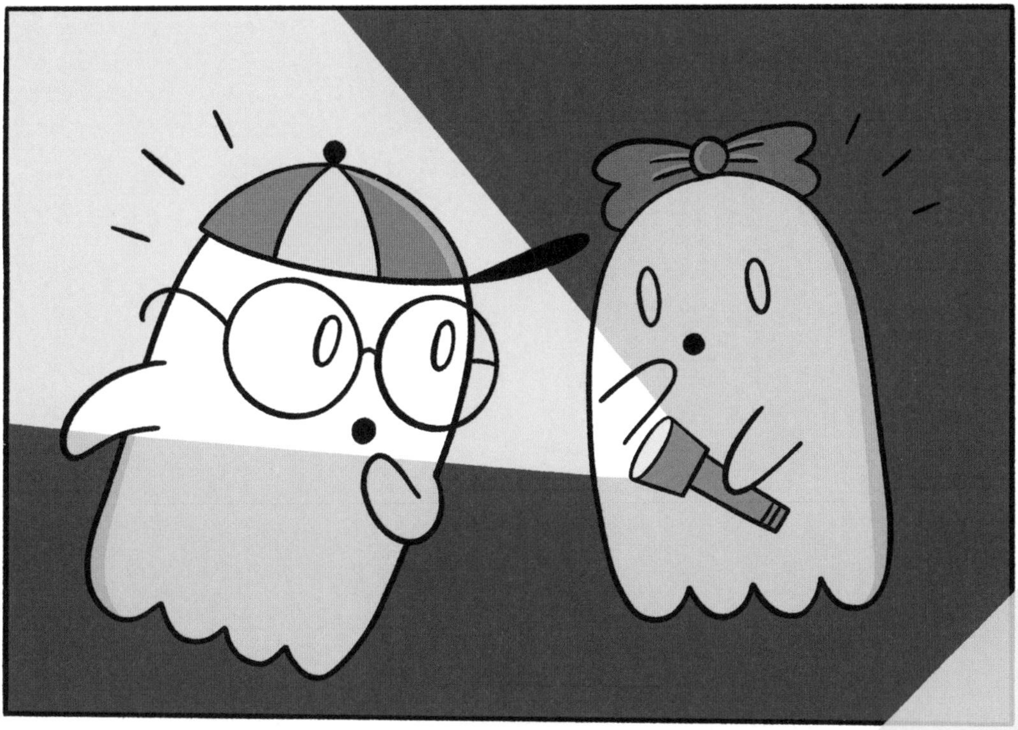

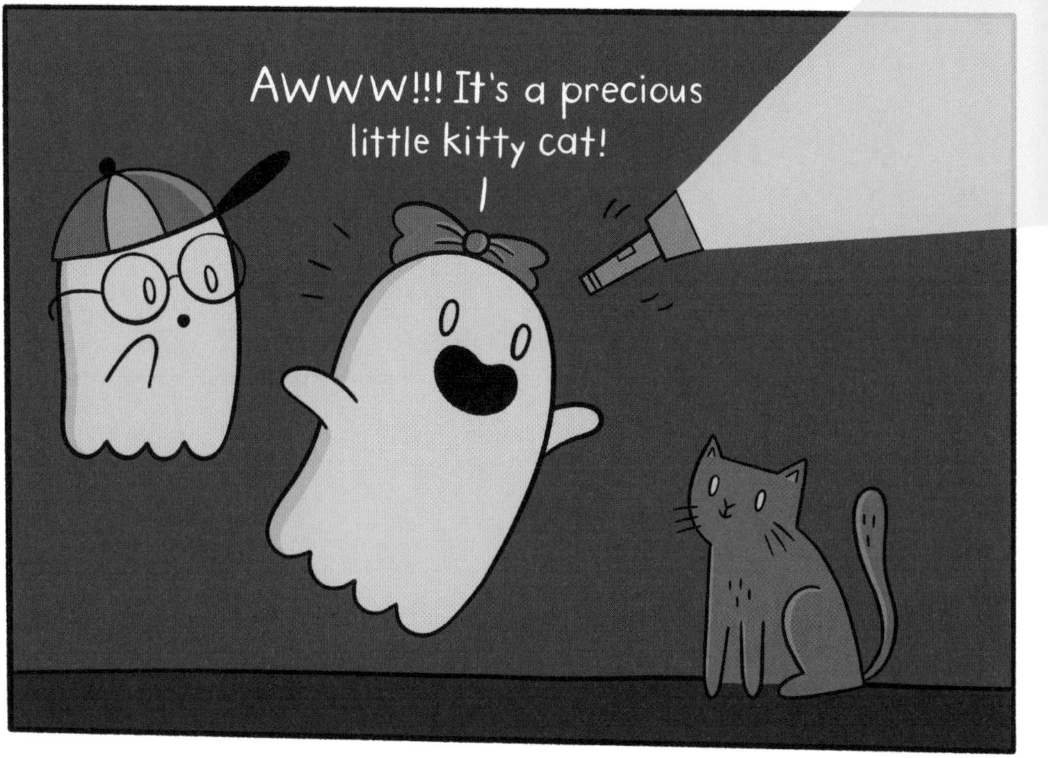
AWWW!!! It's a precious little kitty cat!

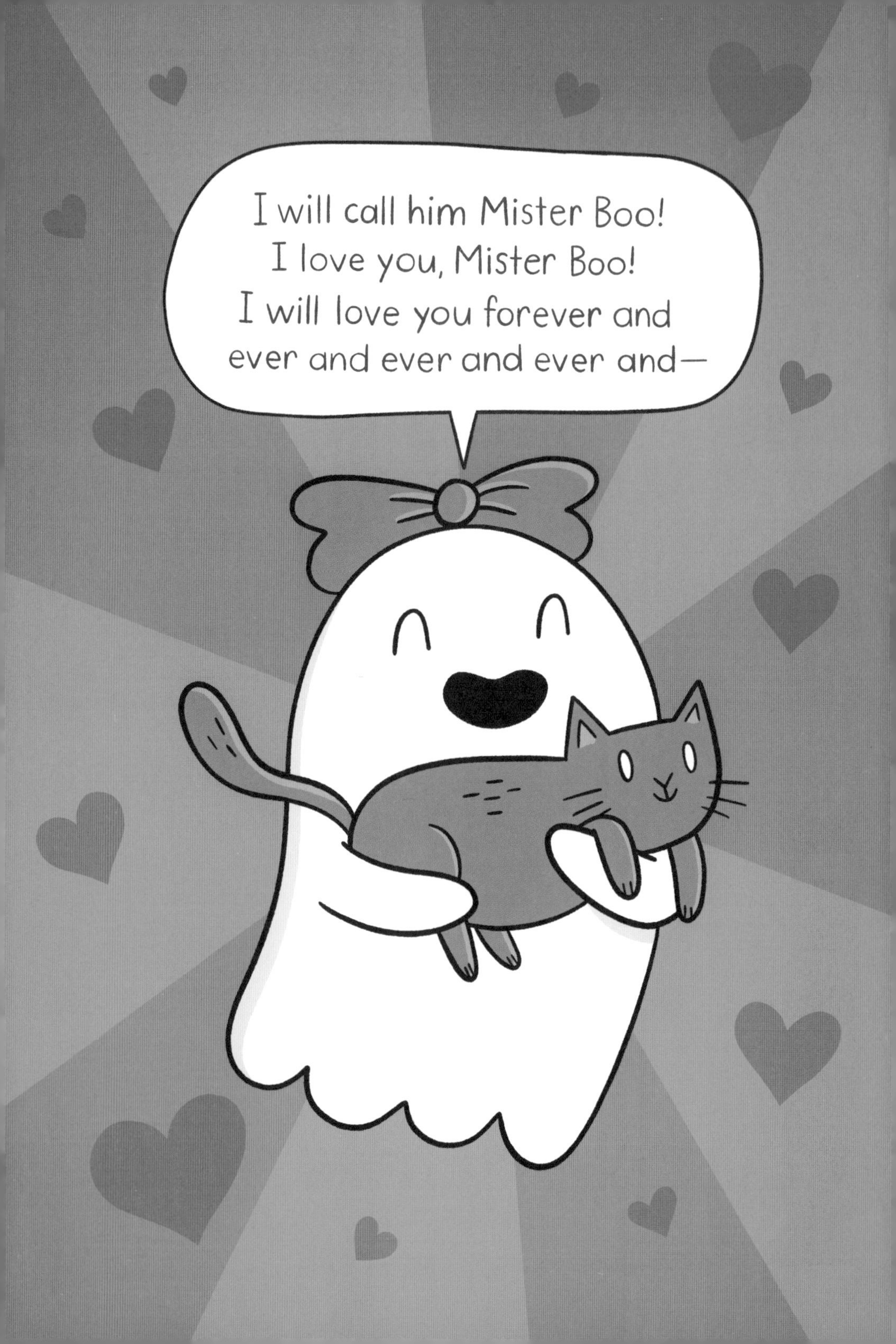
I will call him Mister Boo! I love you, Mister Boo! I will love you forever and ever and ever and ever and—

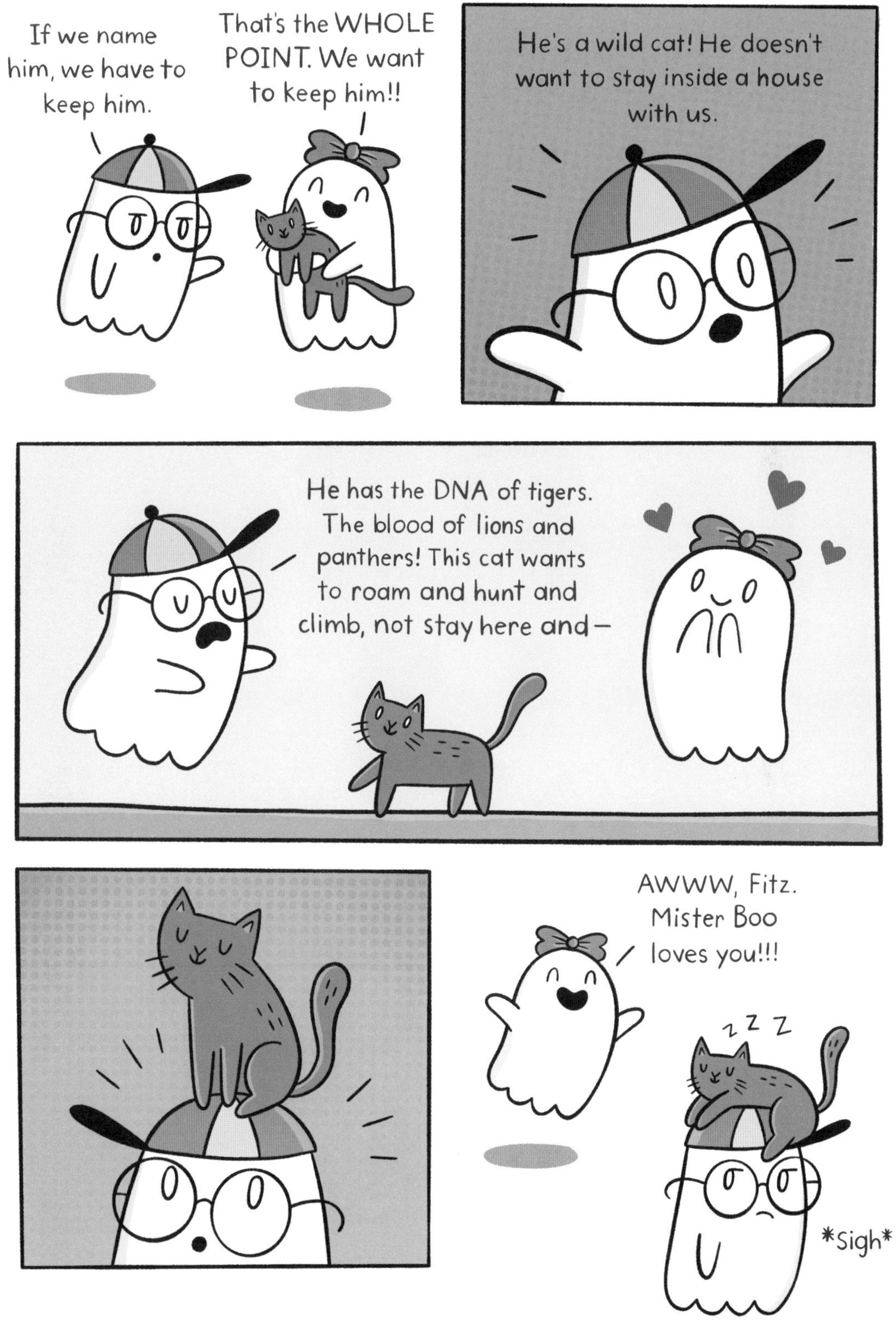
If we name him, we have to keep him.
That's the WHOLE POINT. We want to keep him!!
He's a wild cat! He doesn't want to stay inside a house with us.
He has the DNA of tigers. The blood of lions and panthers! This cat wants to roam and hunt and climb, not stay here and—
AWWW, Fitz. Mister Boo loves you!!!
Z Z Z
*Sigh*

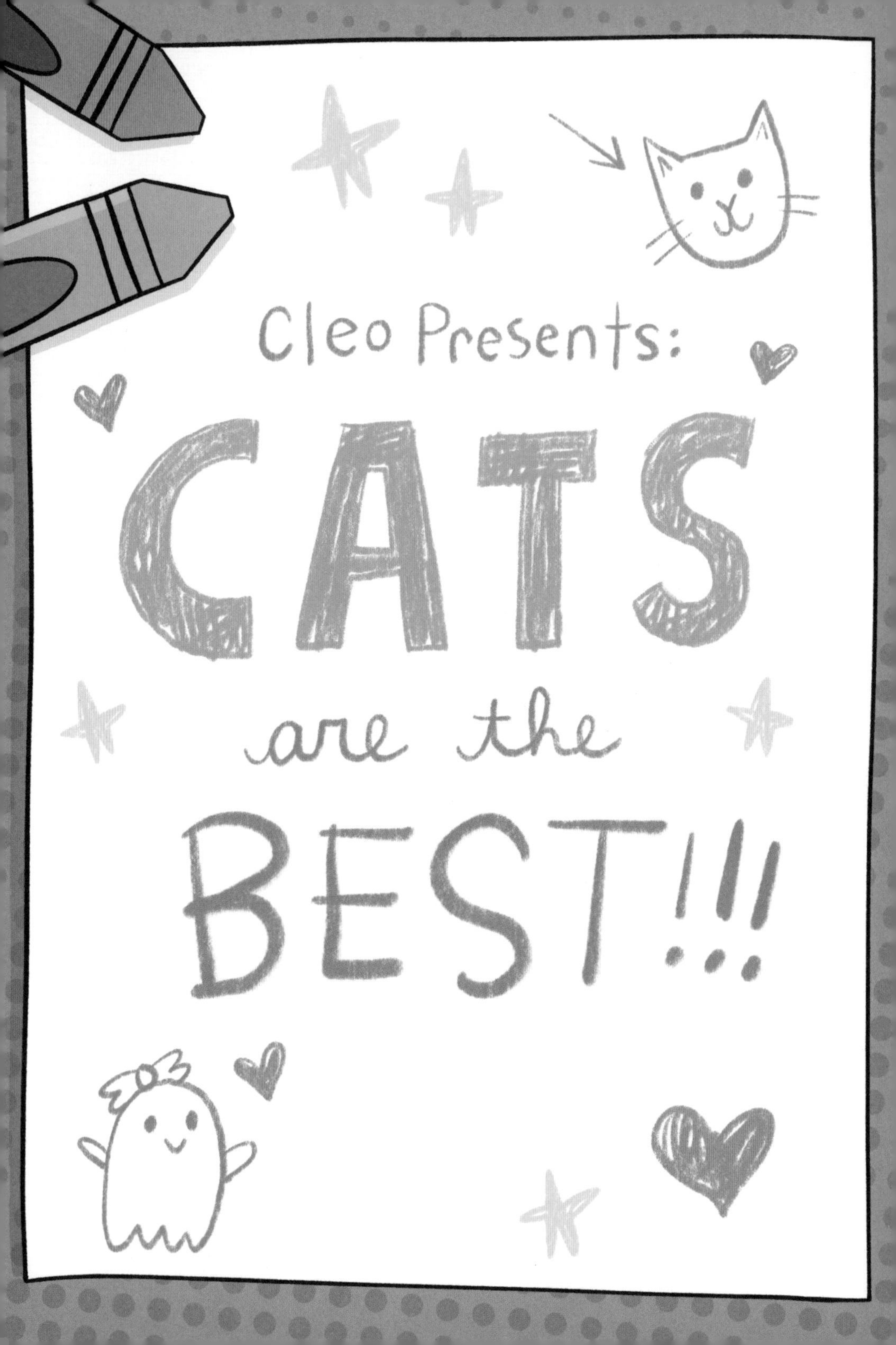
Cleo Presents:
CATS
are the
BEST!!!

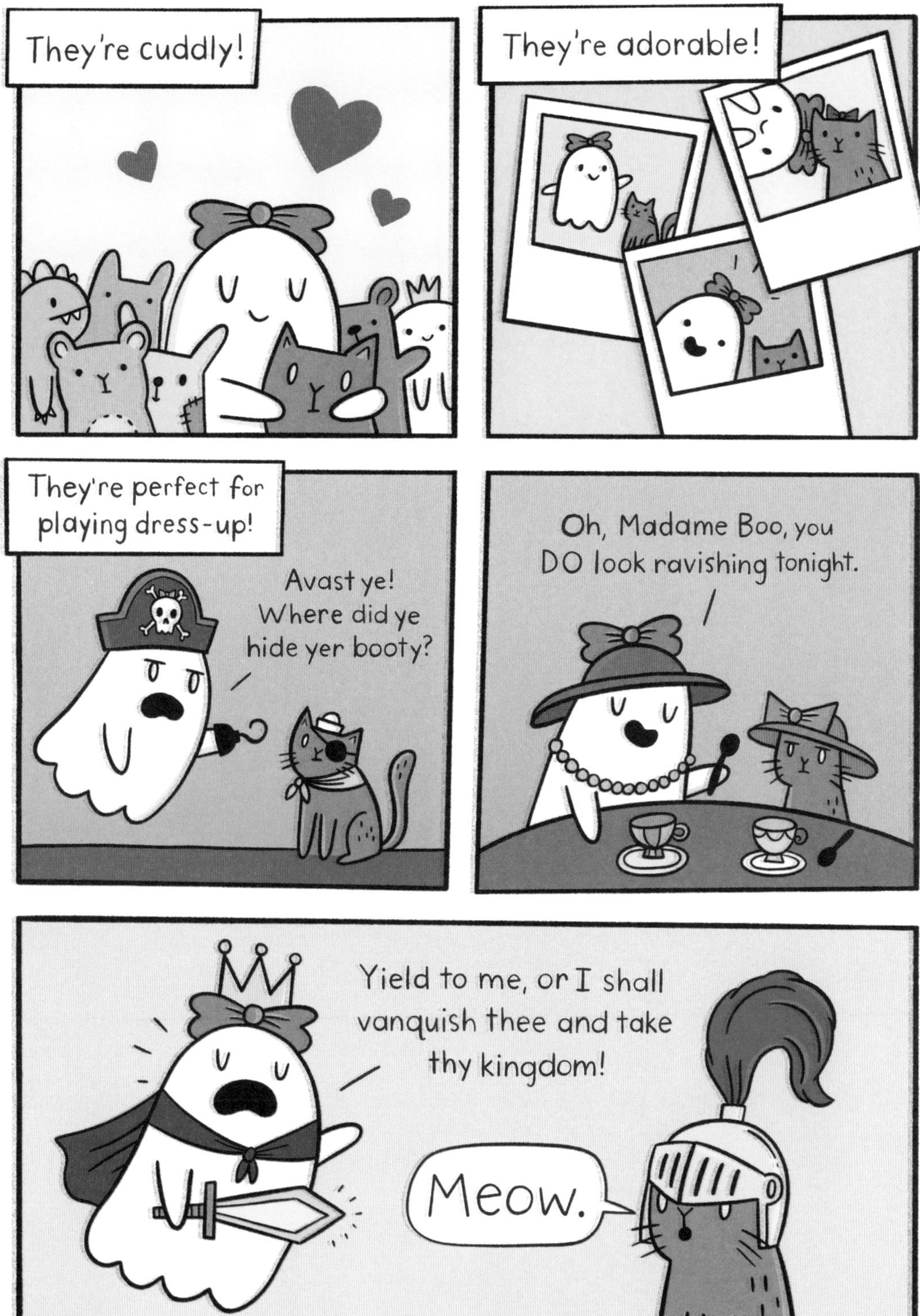
They're cuddly!
They're adorable!
They're perfect for playing dress-up!
Avast ye! Where did ye hide yer booty?
Oh, Madame Boo, you DO look ravishing tonight.
Yield to me, or I shall vanquish thee and take thy kingdom!
Meow.

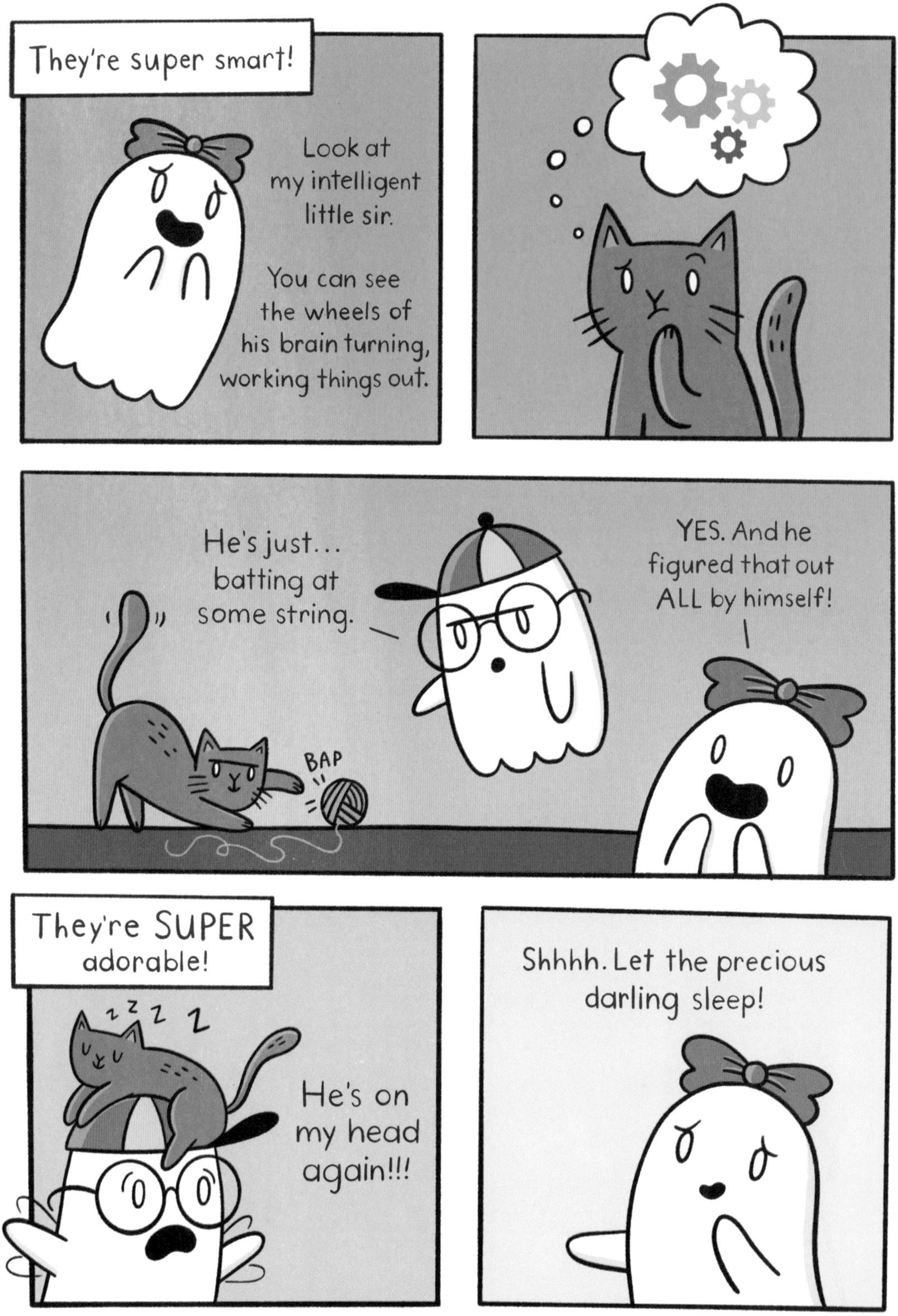
They're super smart!
Look at my intelligent little sir.
You can see the wheels of his brain turning, working things out.
He's just... batting at some string.
BAP
YES. And he figured that out ALL by himself!
They're SUPER adorable!
z z z Z
He's on my head again!!!
Shhhh. Let the precious darling sleep!

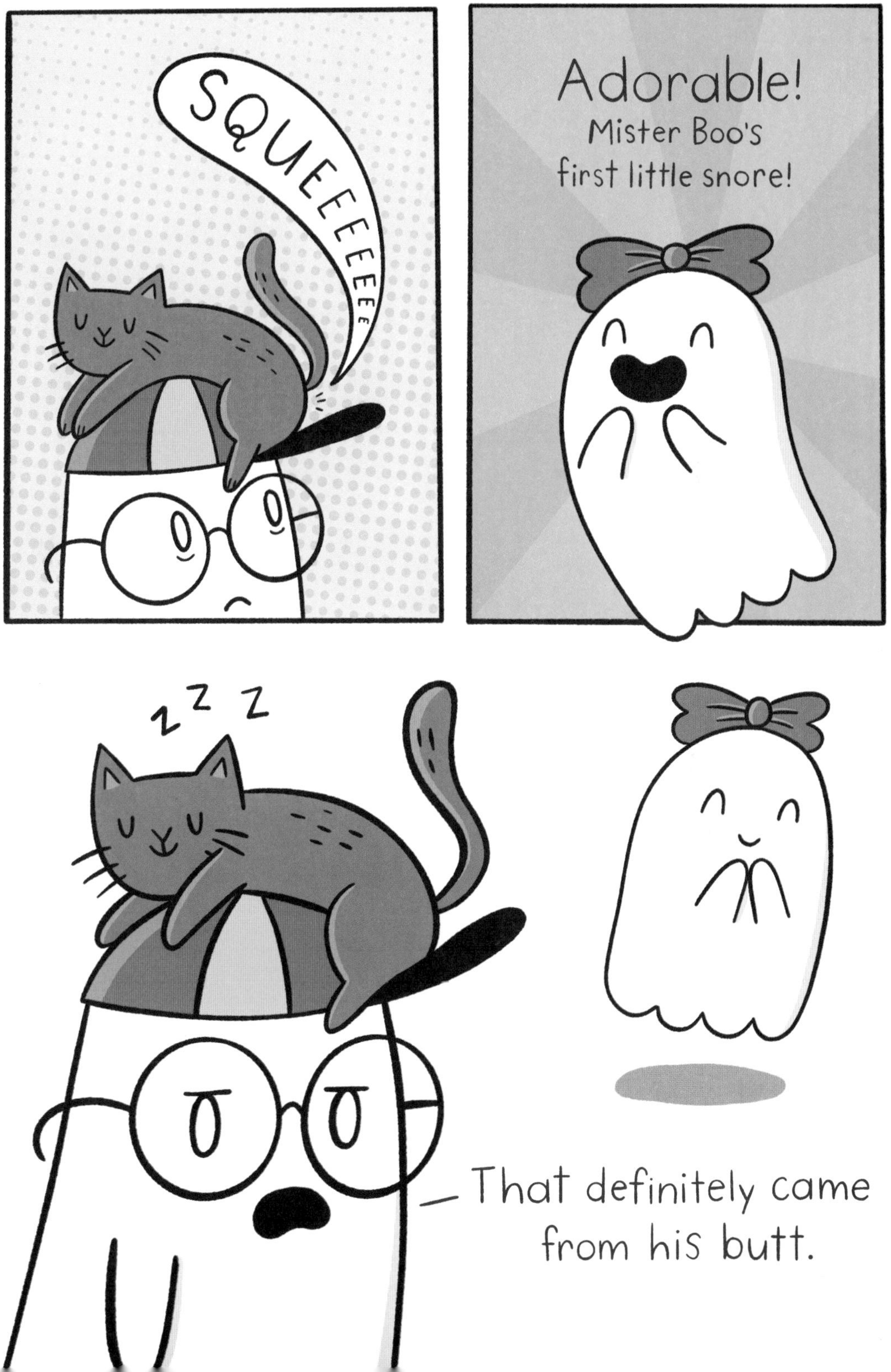
SQUEEEEEEEEEEE
Adorable!
Mister Boo's
first little snore!
Z Z Z
That definitely came
from his butt.

# Catsitting

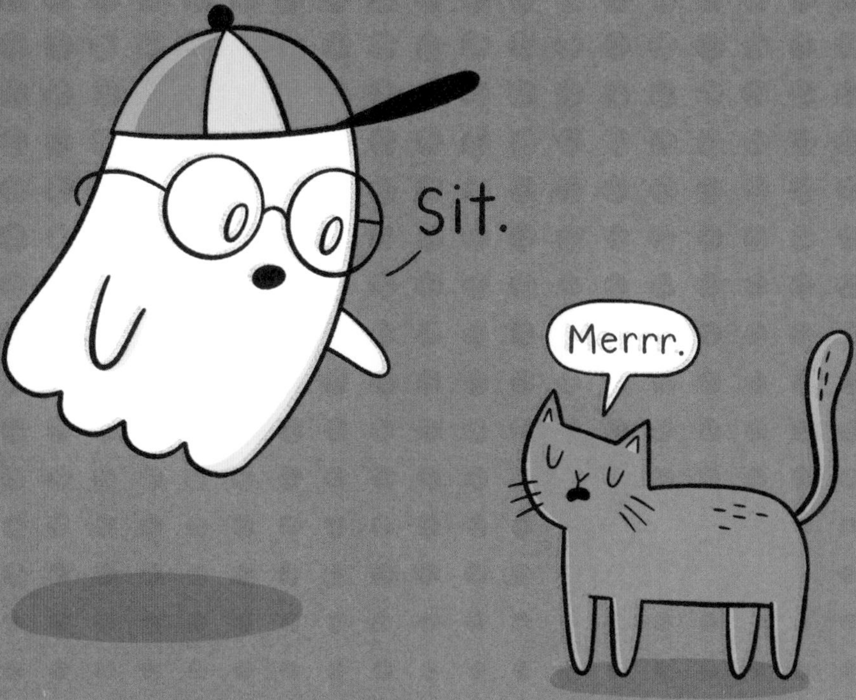
Sit.
Merrr.

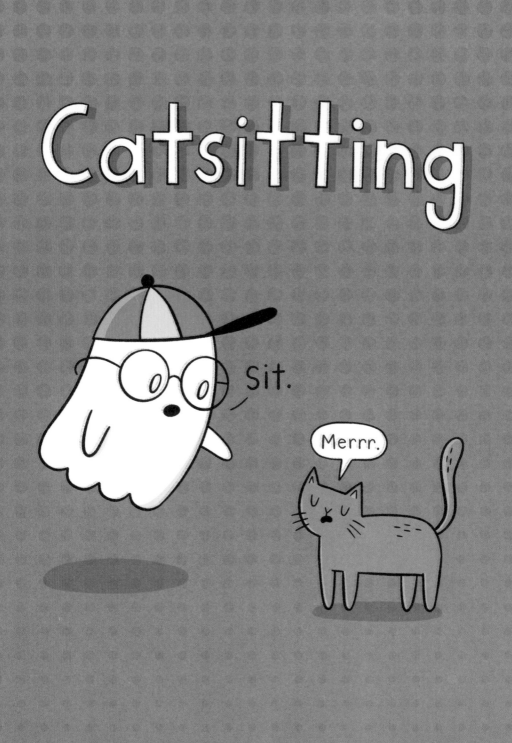

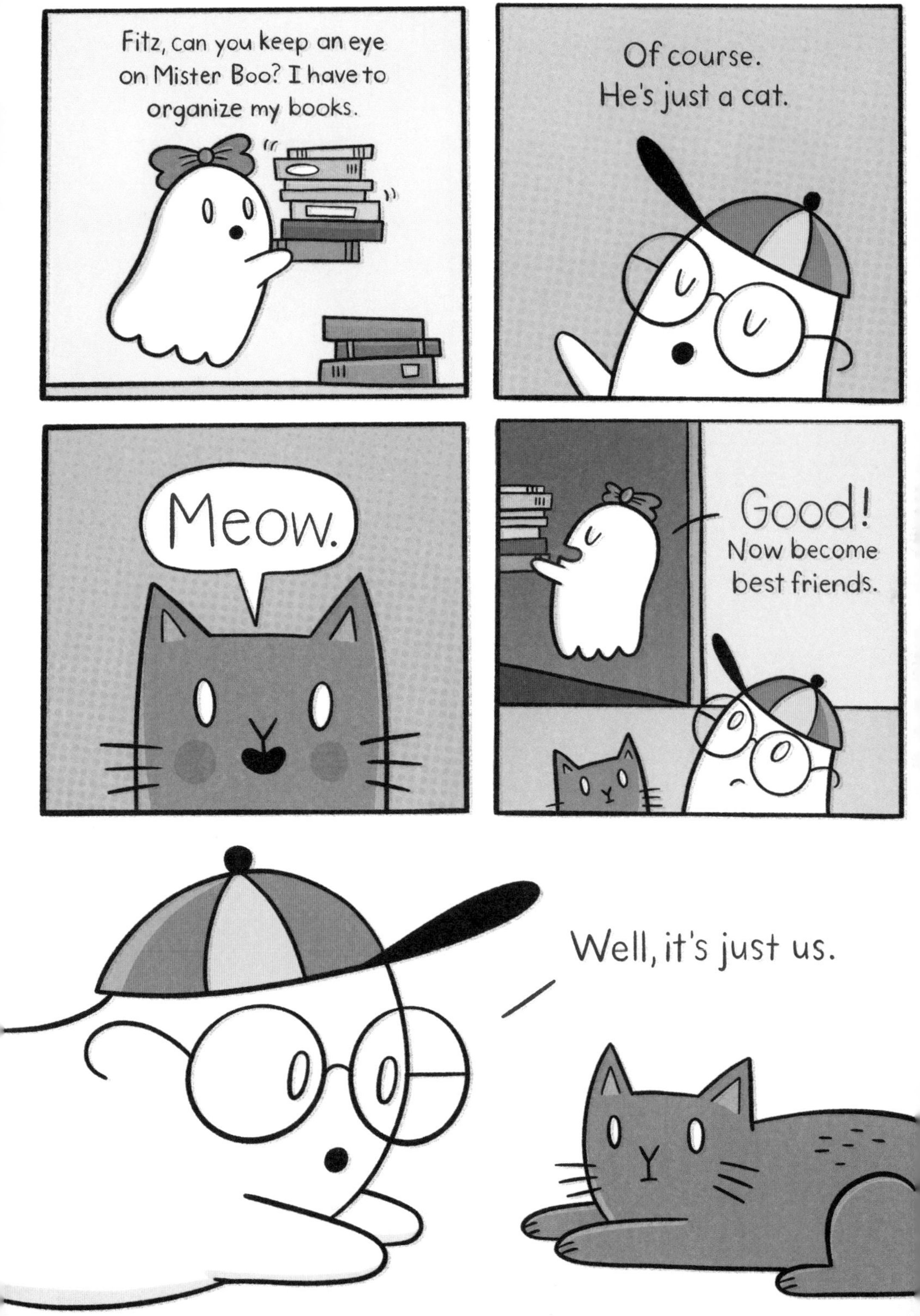
Fitz, can you keep an eye on Mister Boo? I have to organize my books.
Of course. He's just a cat.
Meow.
Good! Now become best friends.
Well, it's just us.

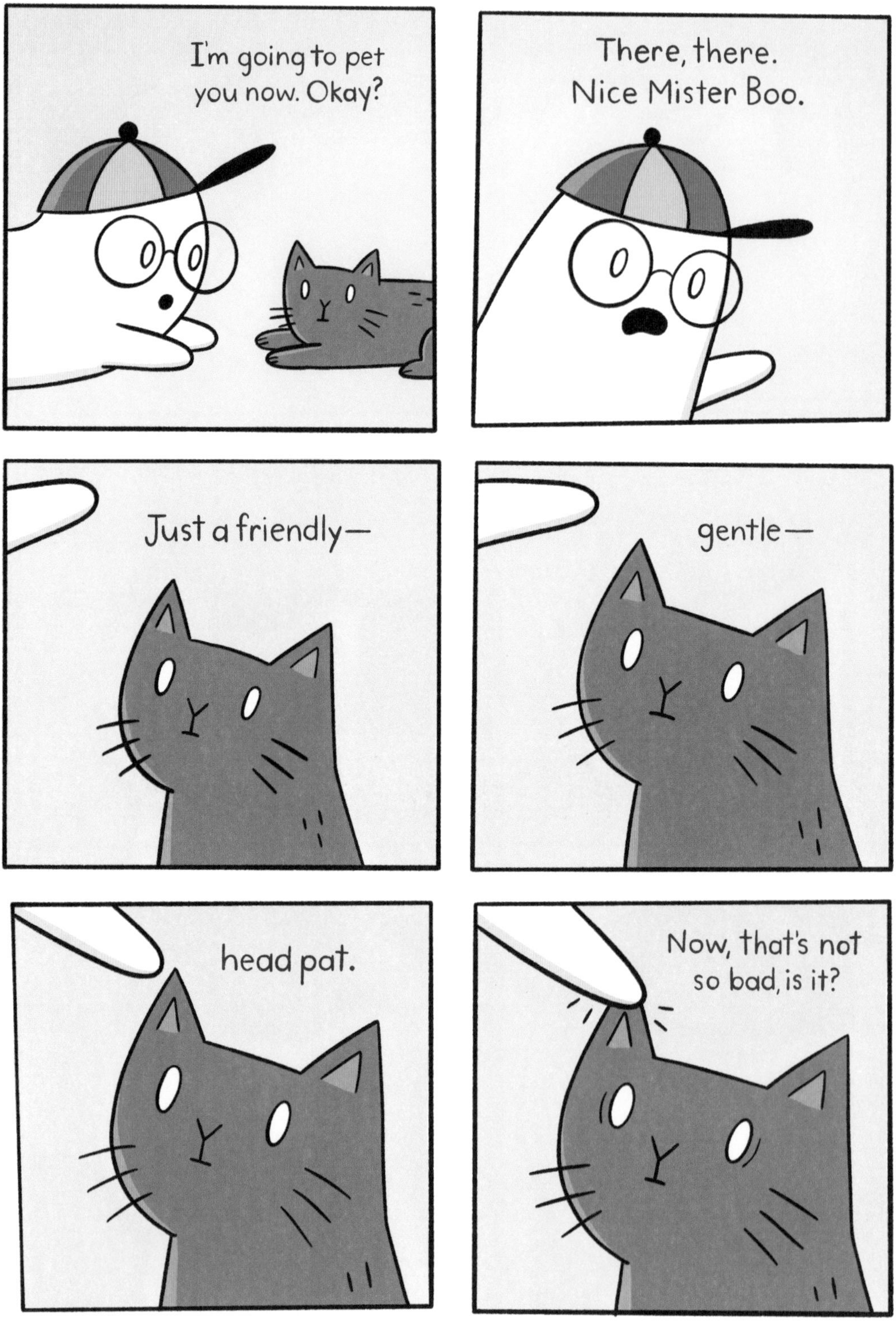
I'm going to pet you now. Okay?
There, there. Nice Mister Boo.
Just a friendly—
gentle—
head pat.
Now, that's not so bad, is it?

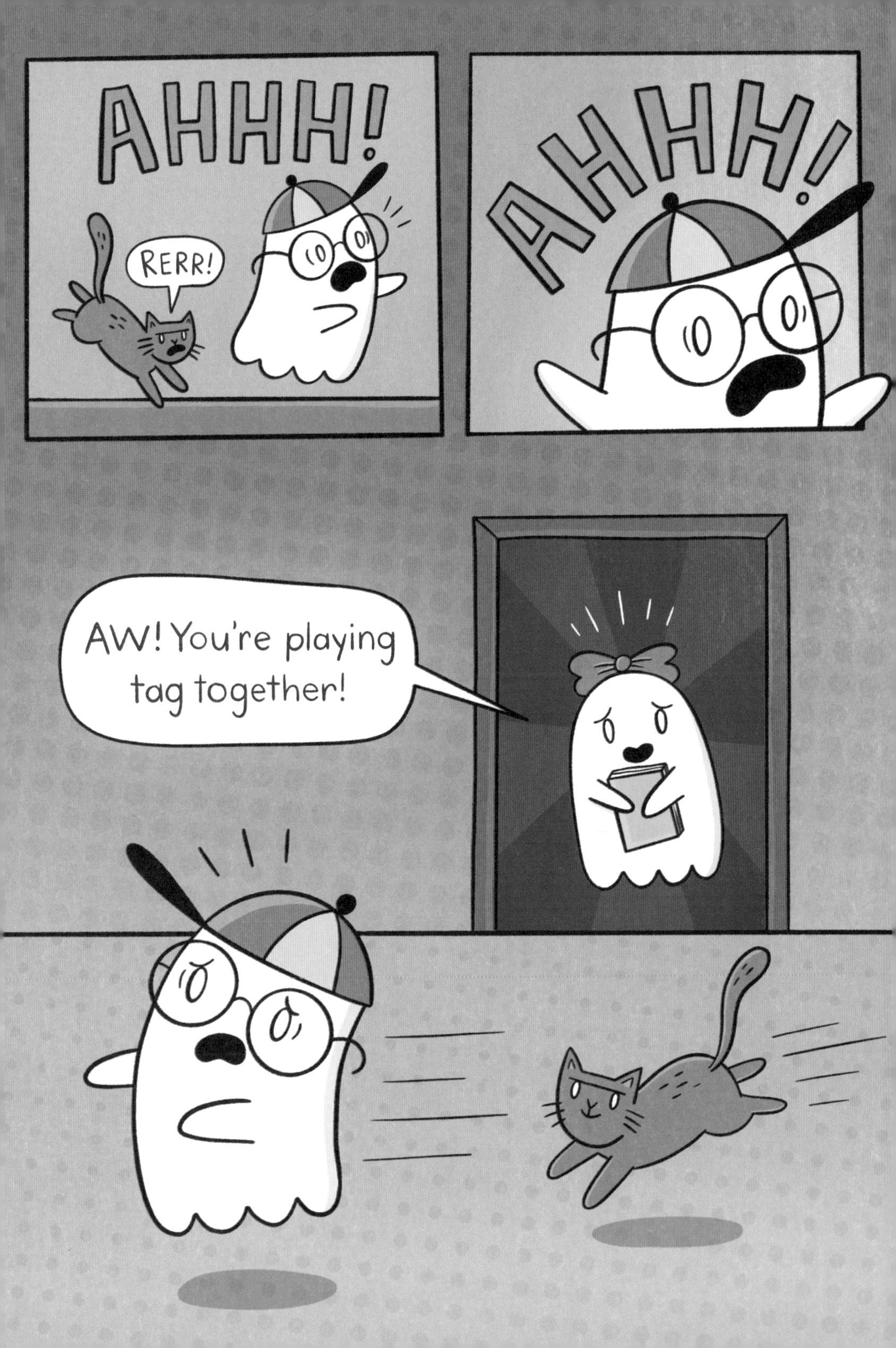
AHHH!
RERR!
AHHH!
AW! You're playing tag together!

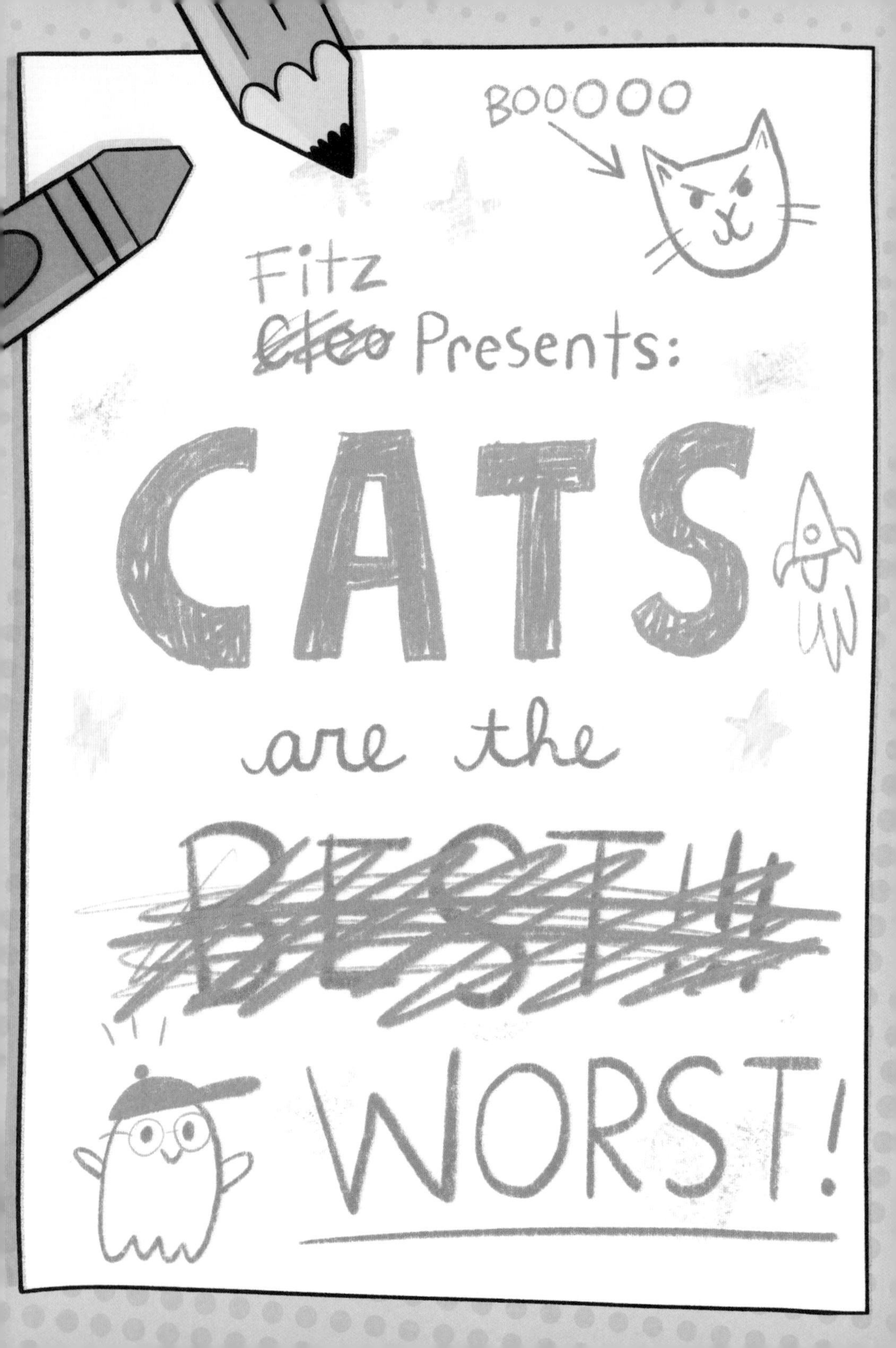
BOOOOO
~~Cleo~~ Fitz Presents:
CATS
are the
~~BEST!!~~
WORST!

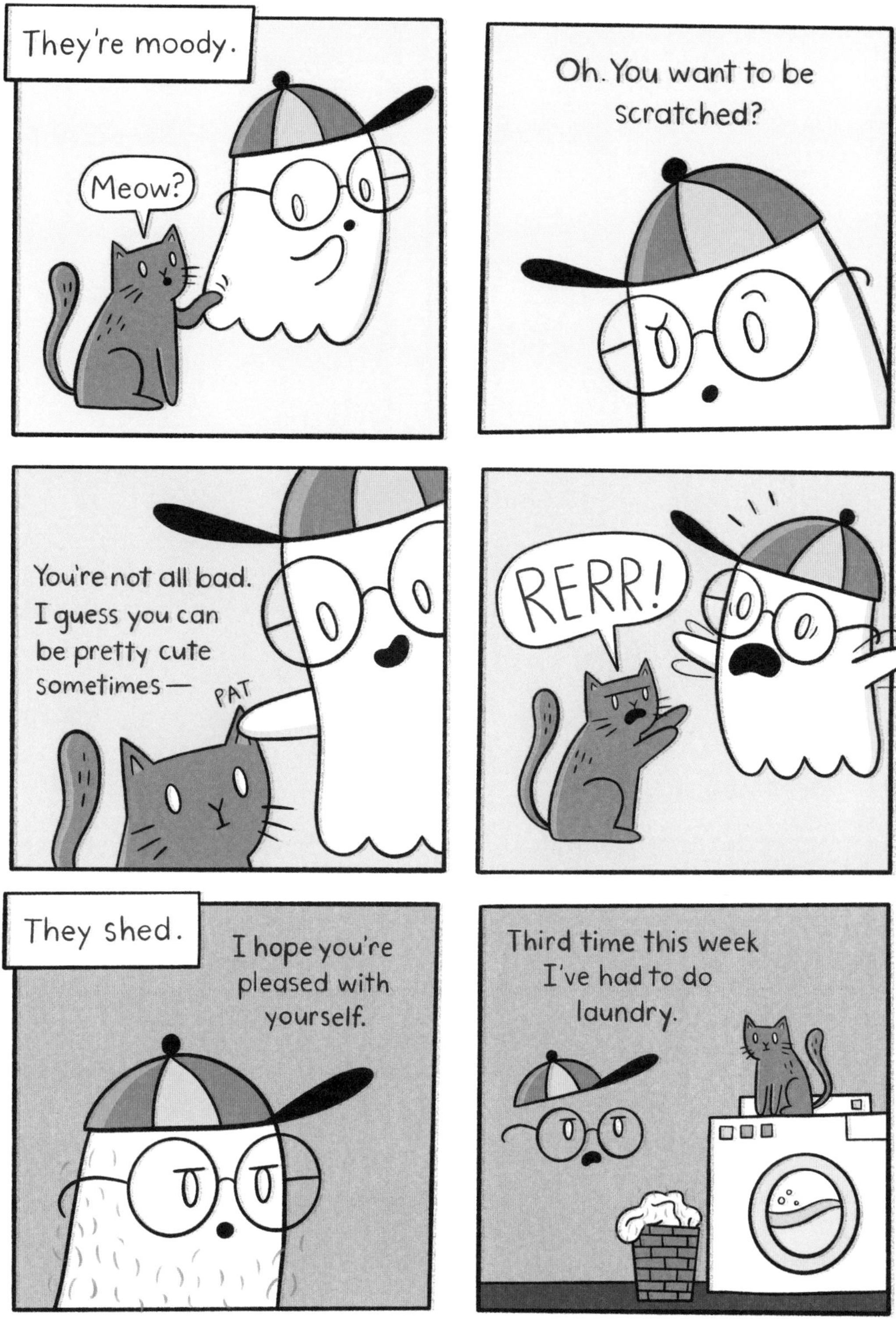
They're moody.
Meow?
Oh. You want to be scratched?
You're not all bad. I guess you can be pretty cute sometimes—
PAT
RERR!
They shed.
I hope you're pleased with yourself.
Third time this week I've had to do laundry.

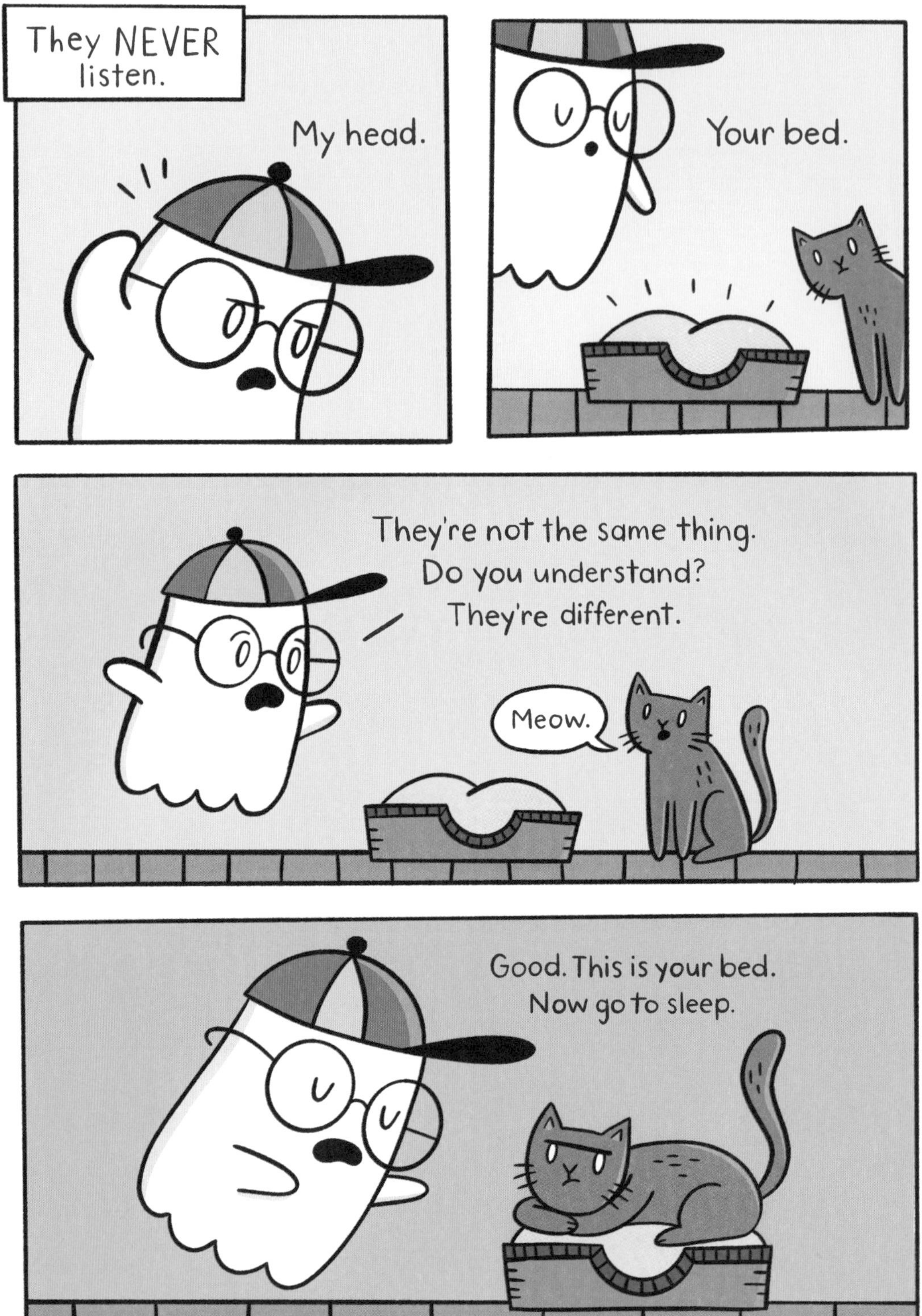
They NEVER listen.
My head.
Your bed.
They're not the same thing. Do you understand? They're different.
Meow.
Good. This is your bed. Now go to sleep.

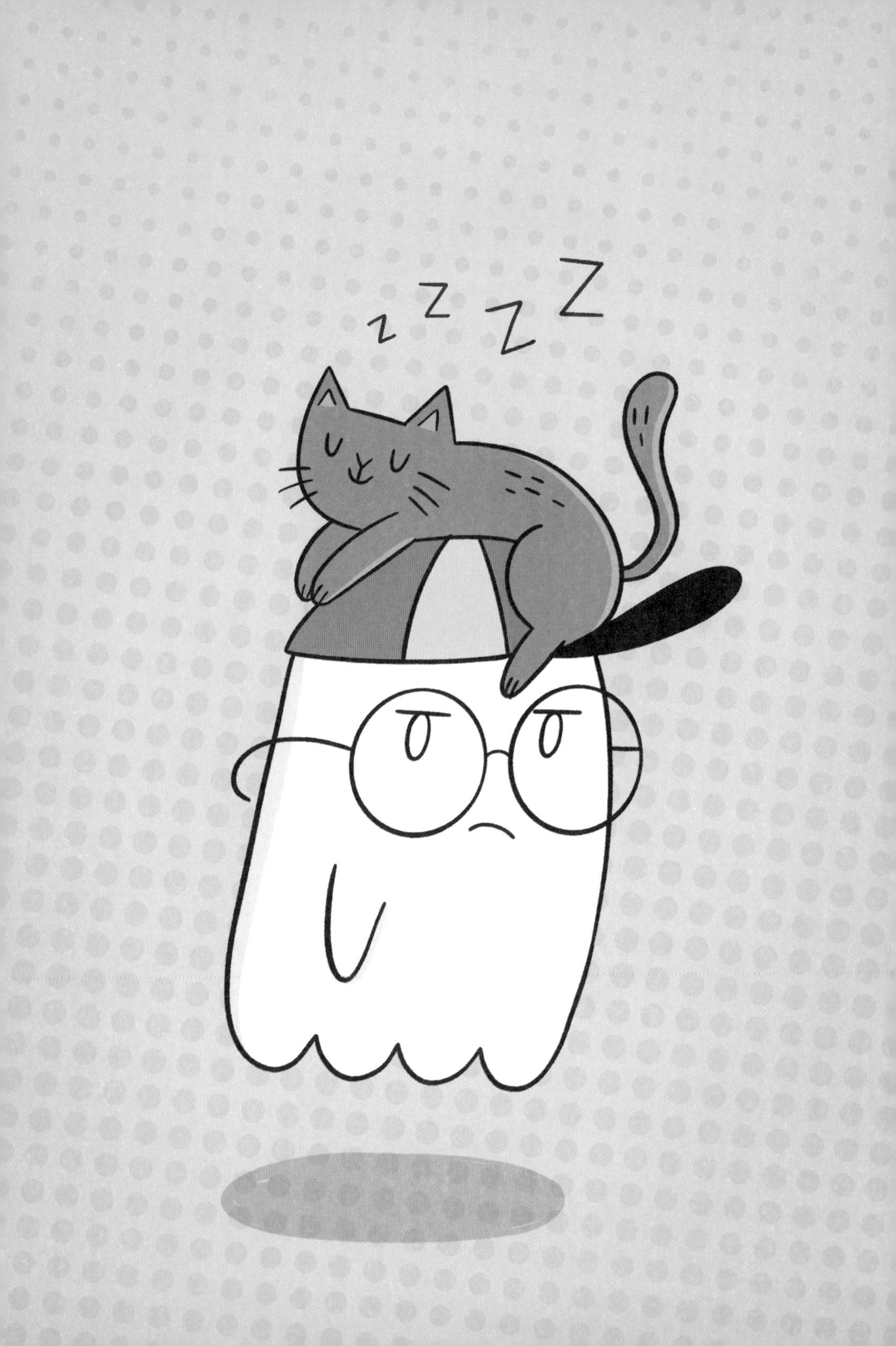
z z Z Z

# Beach Day

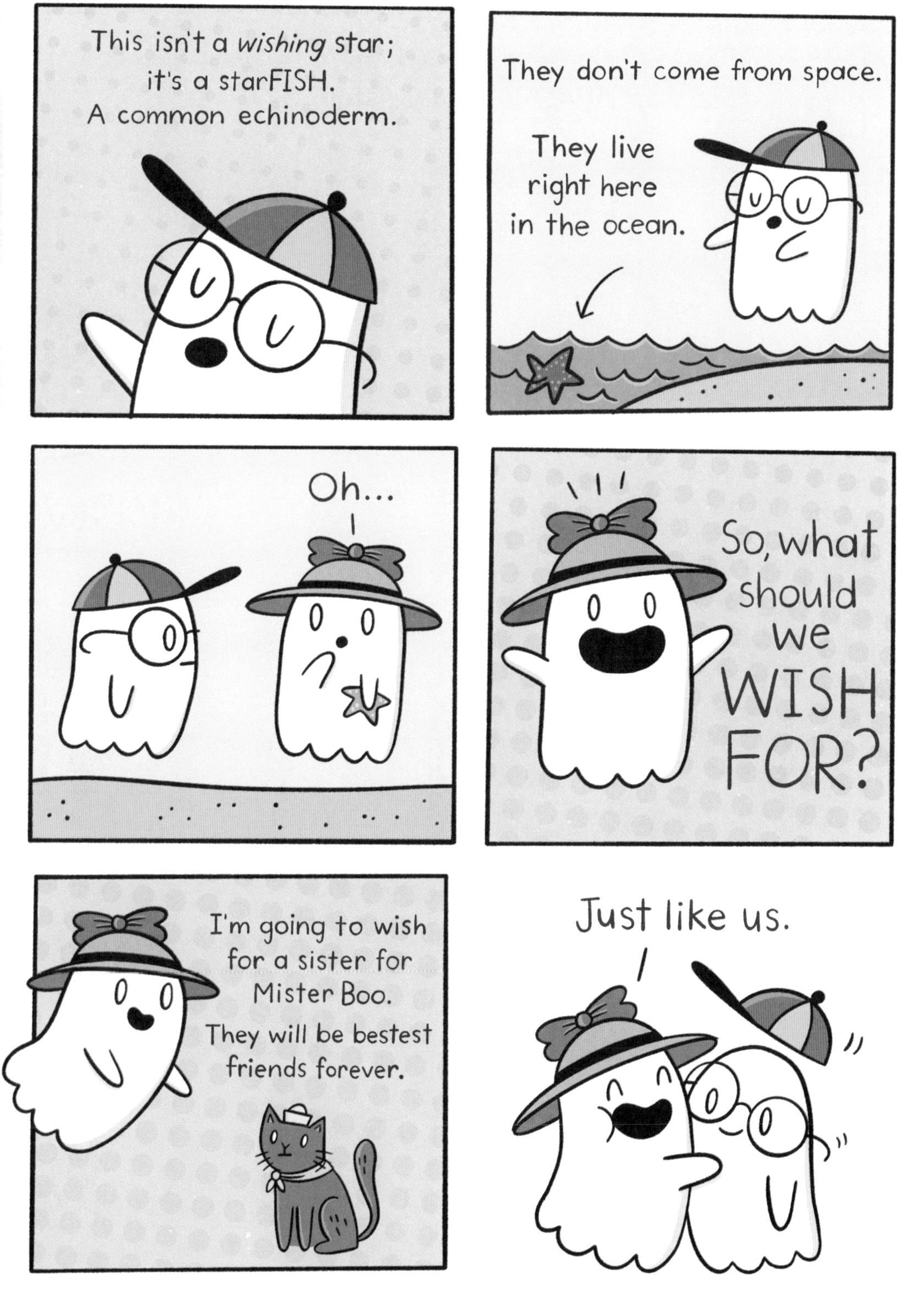
This isn't a *wishing* star;
it's a starFISH.
A common echinoderm.
They don't come from space.
They live
right here
in the ocean.
Oh...
So, what
should
we
WISH
FOR?
I'm going to wish
for a sister for
Mister Boo.
They will be bestest
friends forever.
Just like us.

# We ALL Scream

ICE CREAM

ICE CREAM!!

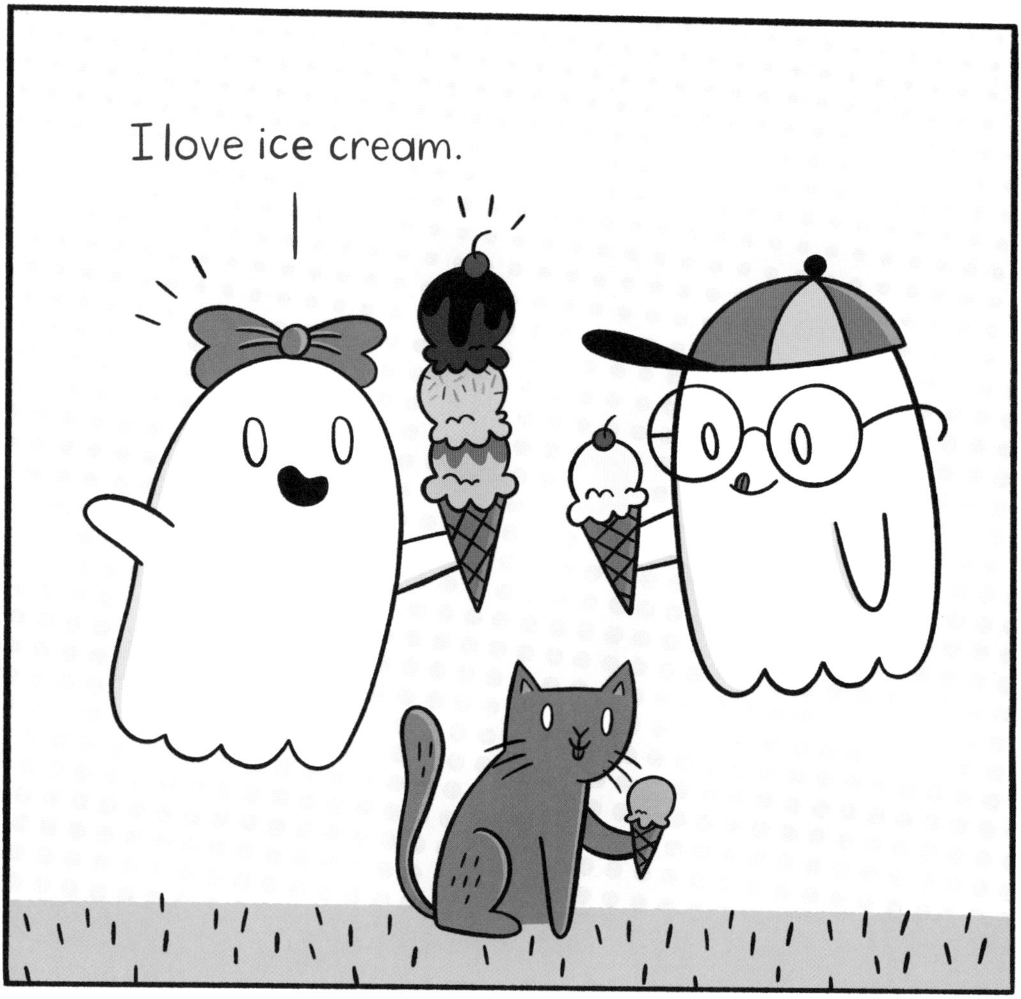
I love ice cream.

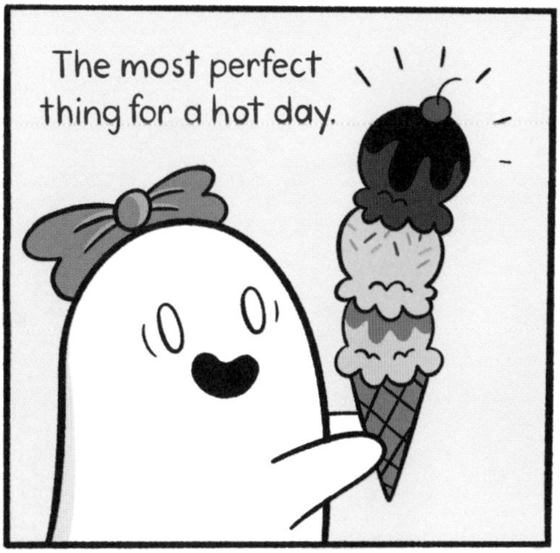
The most perfect
thing for a hot day.

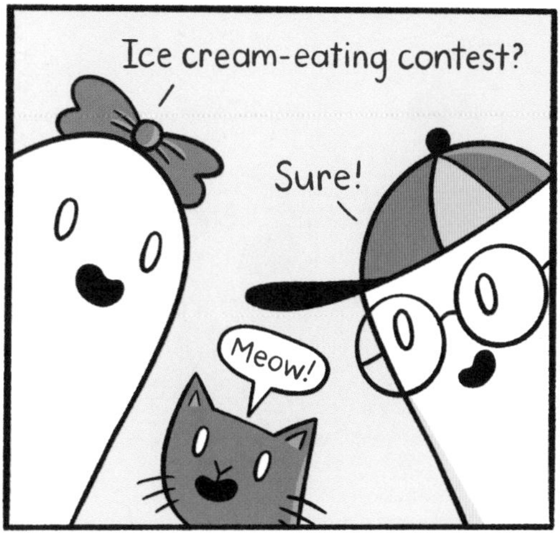
Ice cream-eating contest?
Sure!
Meow!

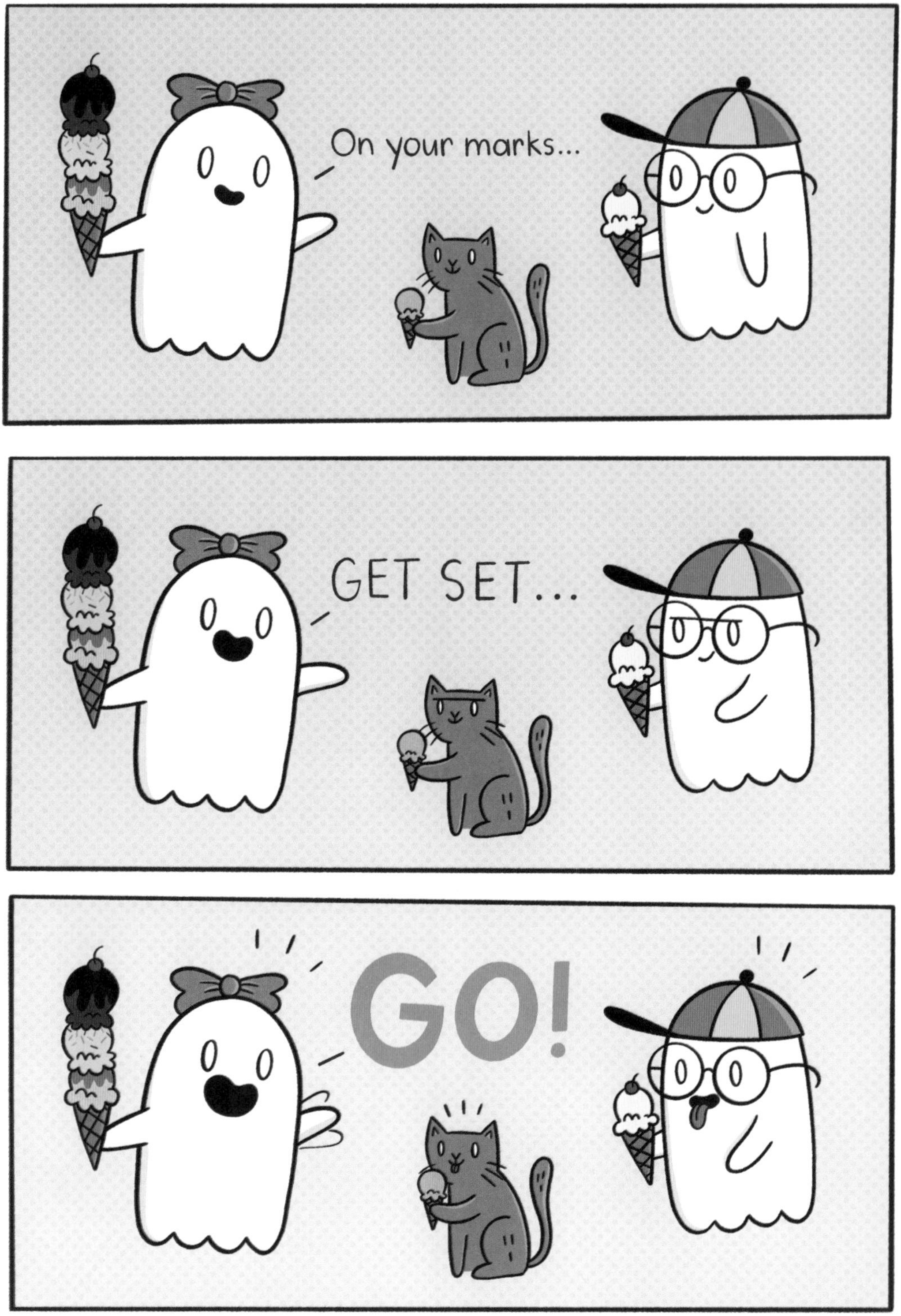
On your marks...
GET SET...
GO!

LICK LICK
CHOMP LICK

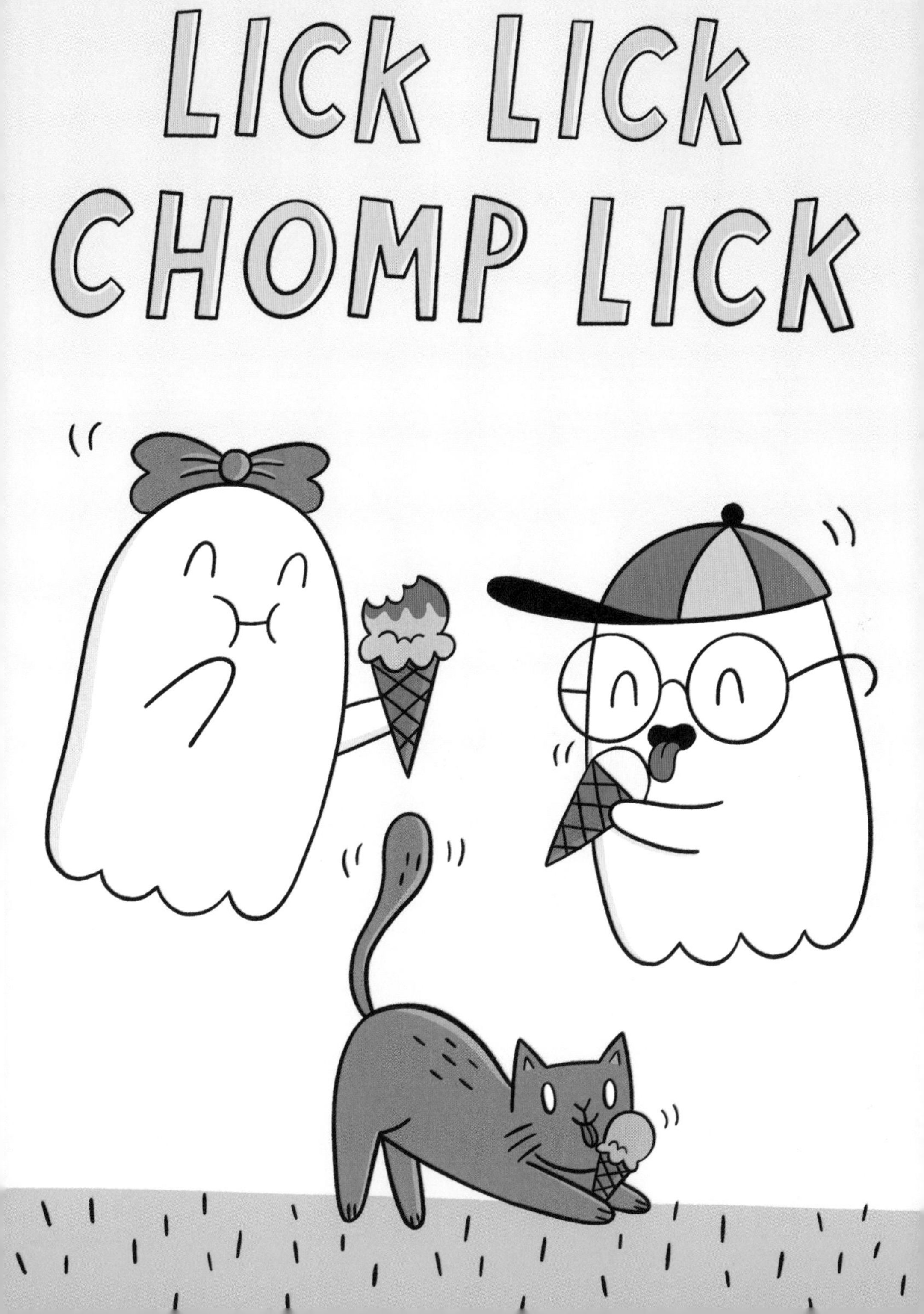

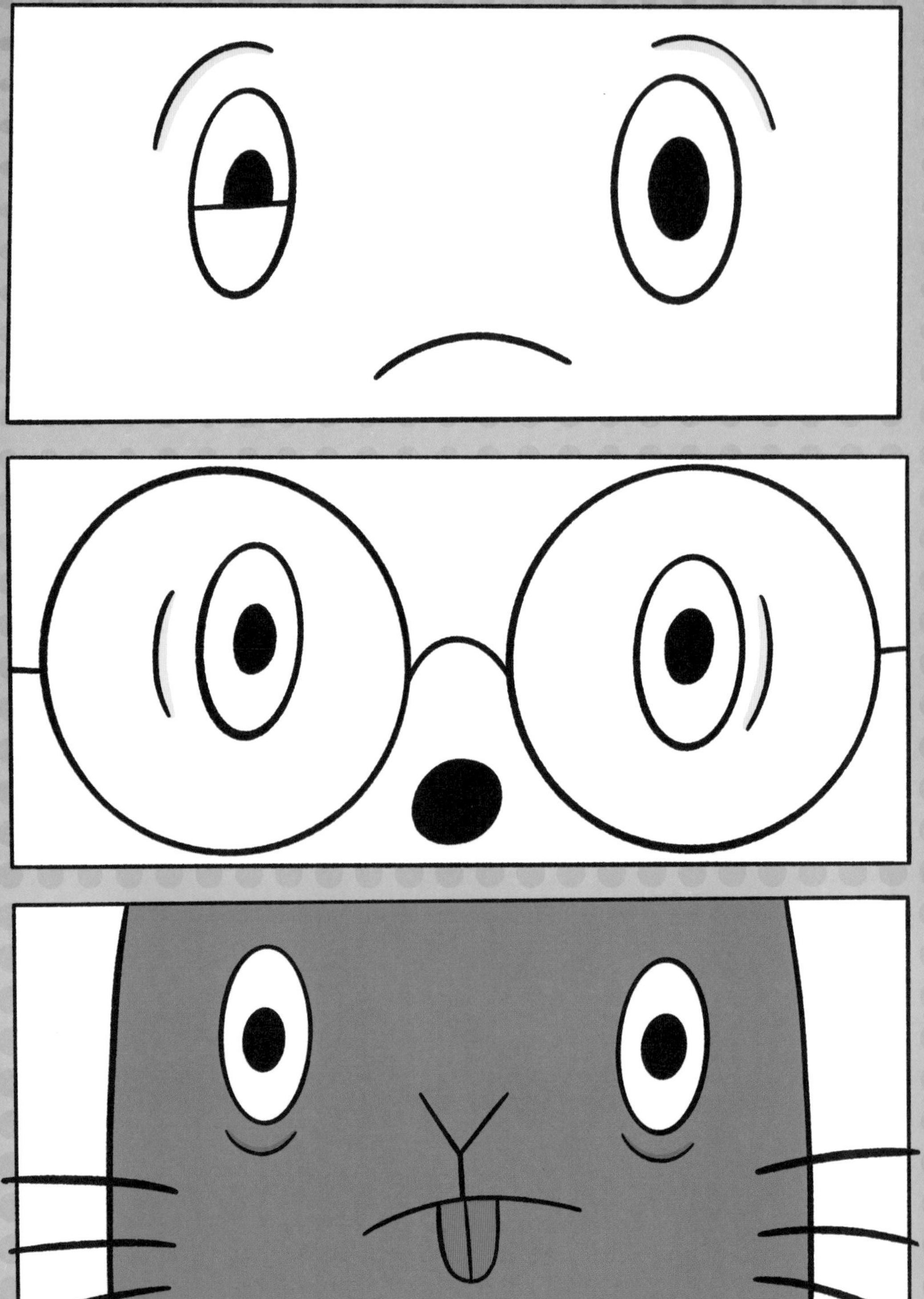

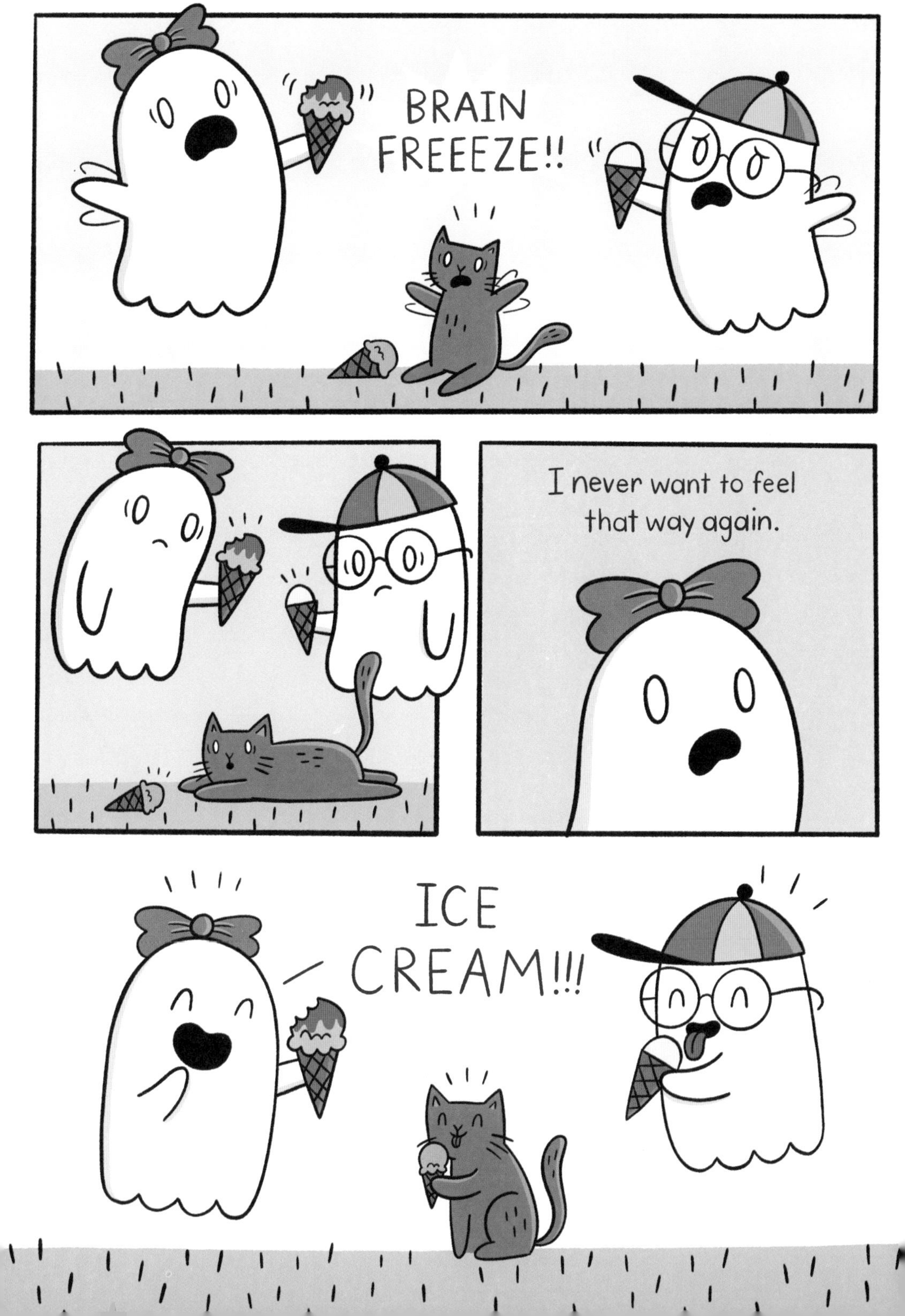
BRAIN FREEEZE!!
I never want to feel that way again.
ICE CREAM!!!

# Paper Planes

For the loop-de-loop world record, she needs... SEVEN LOOPS.

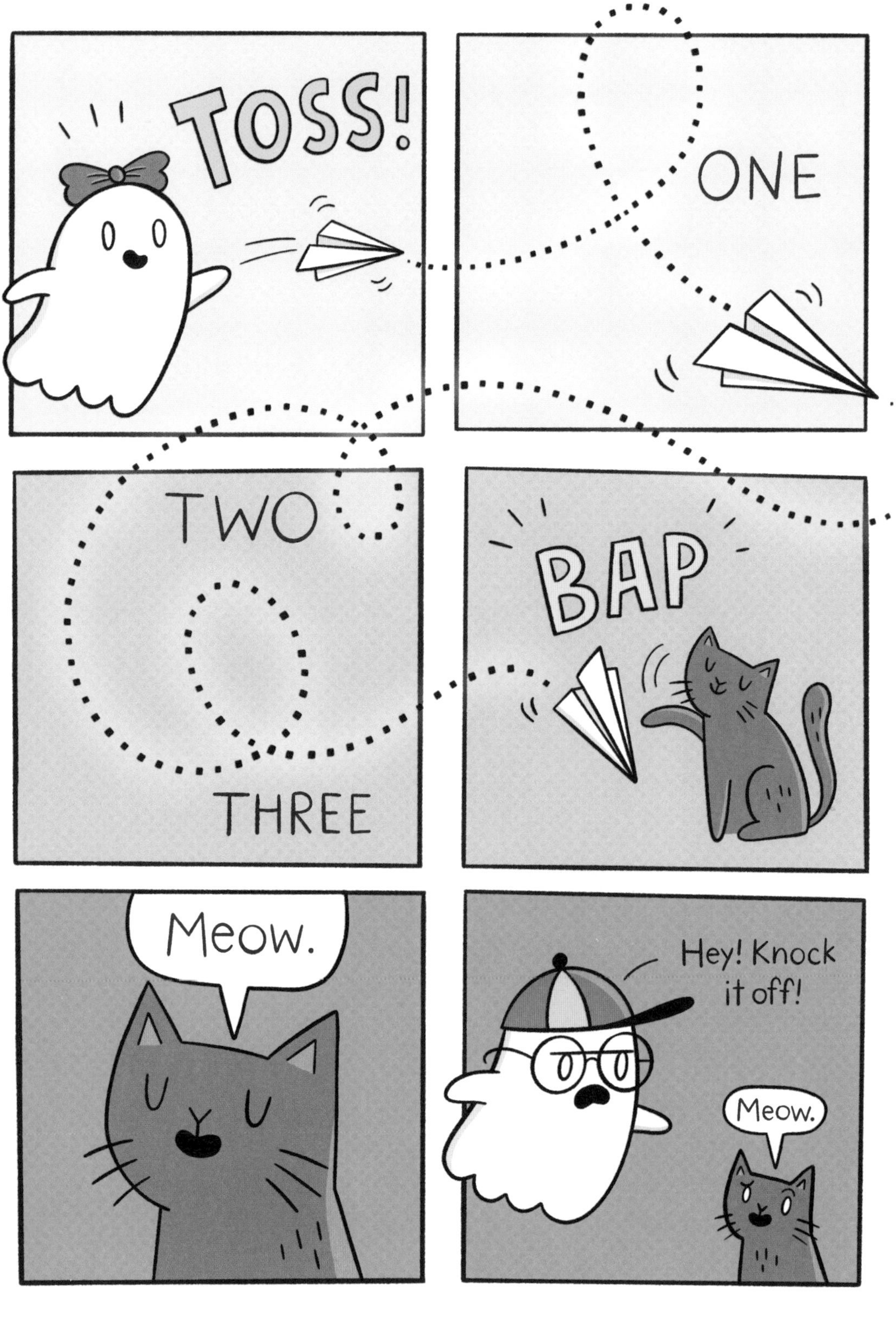
TOSS!
ONE
TWO
THREE
BAP
Meow.
Hey! Knock it off!
Meow.

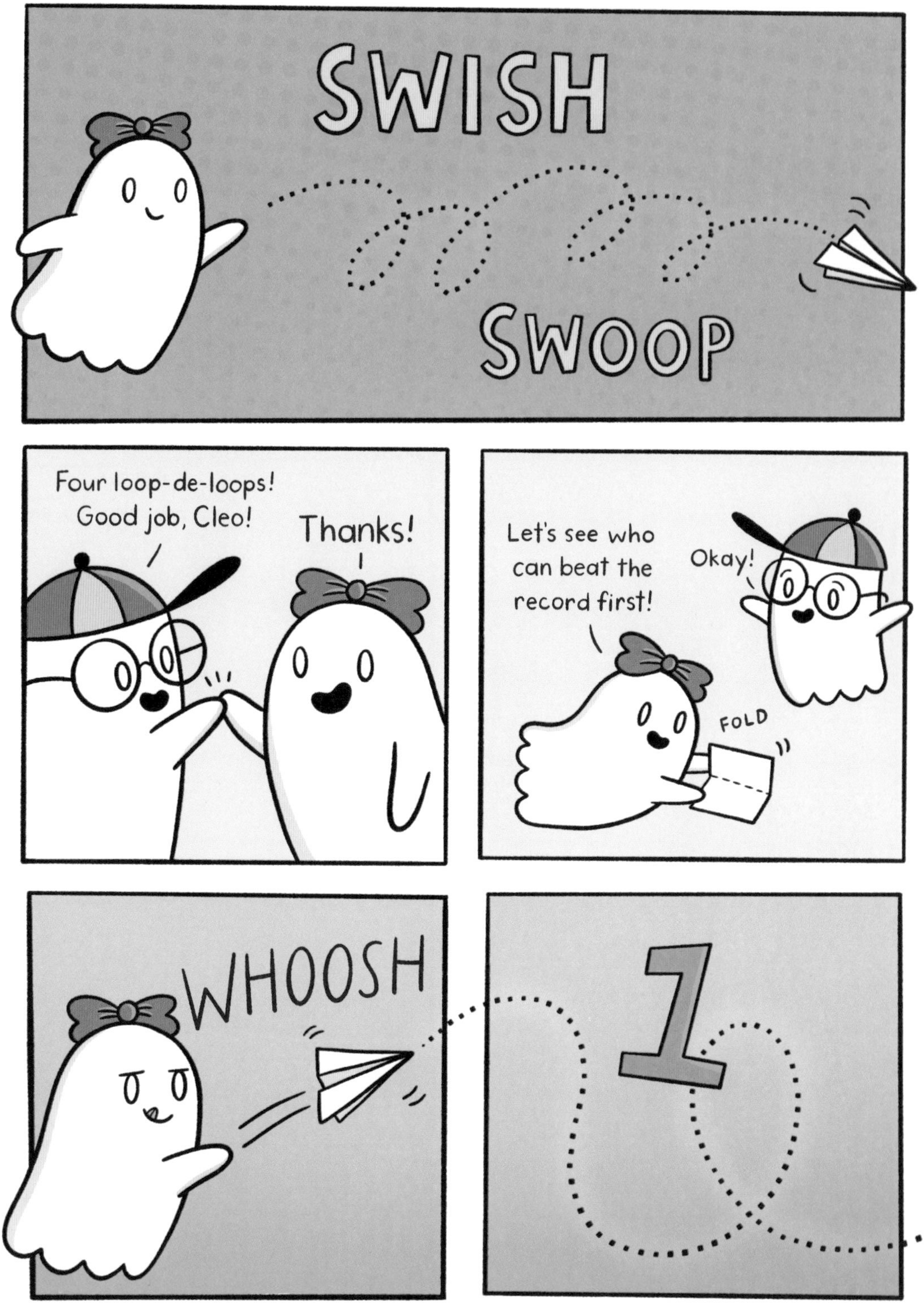
SWISH
SWOOP
Four loop-de-loops! Good job, Cleo!
Thanks!
Let's see who can beat the record first!
Okay!
FOLD
WHOOSH
1

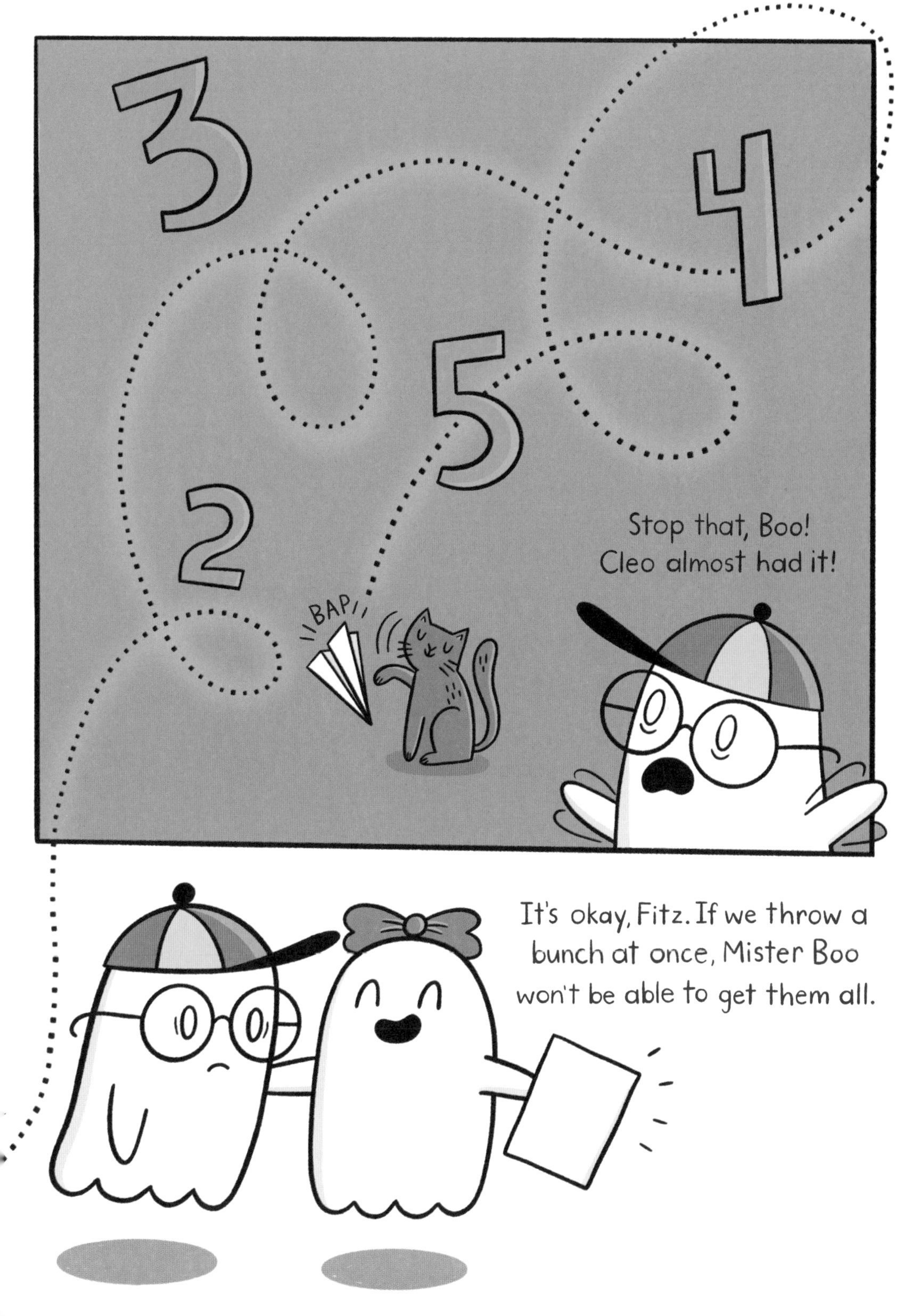
3
4
5
2
BAP
Stop that, Boo!
Cleo almost had it!
It's okay, Fitz. If we throw a
bunch at once, Mister Boo
won't be able to get them all.

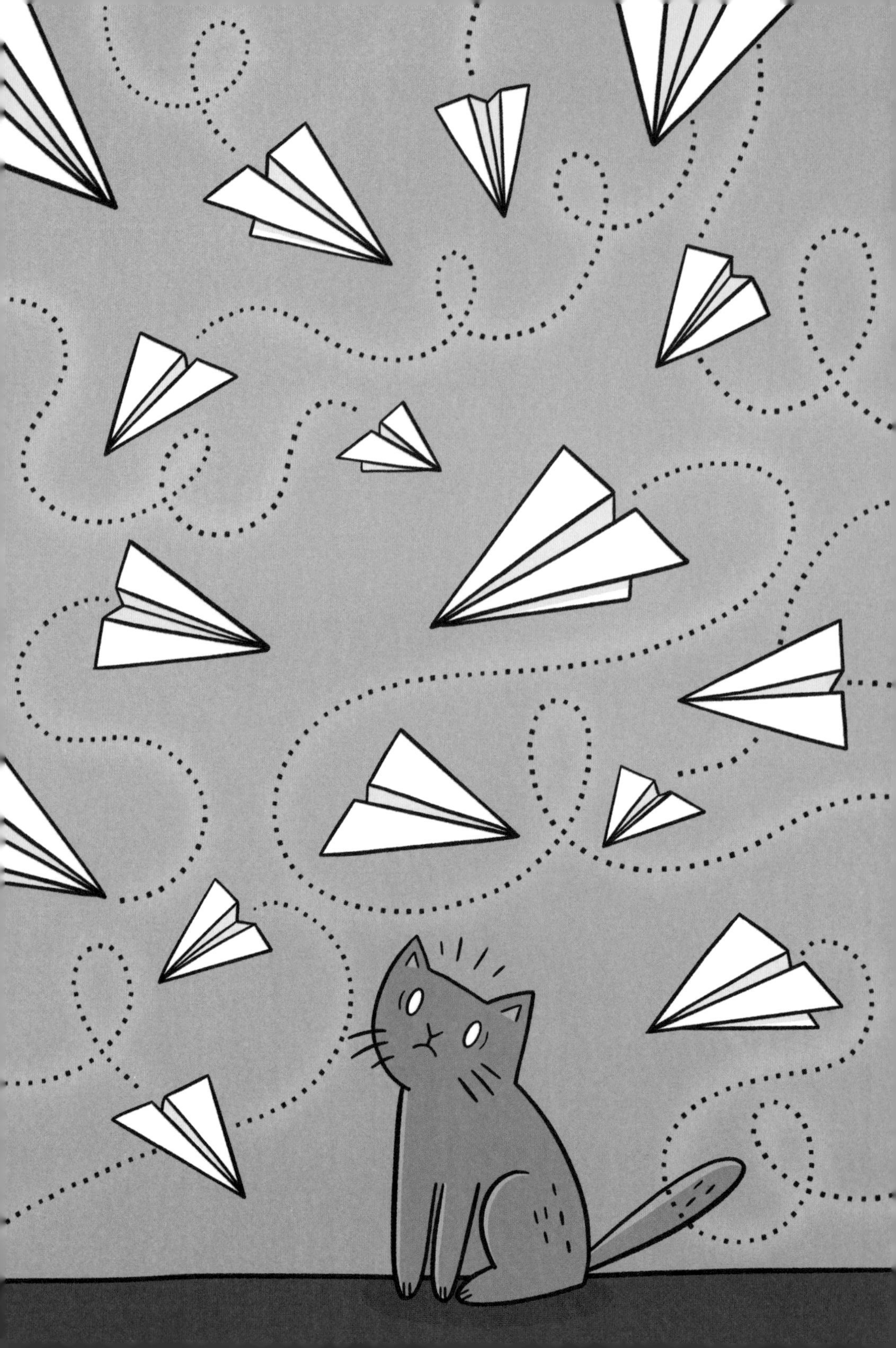

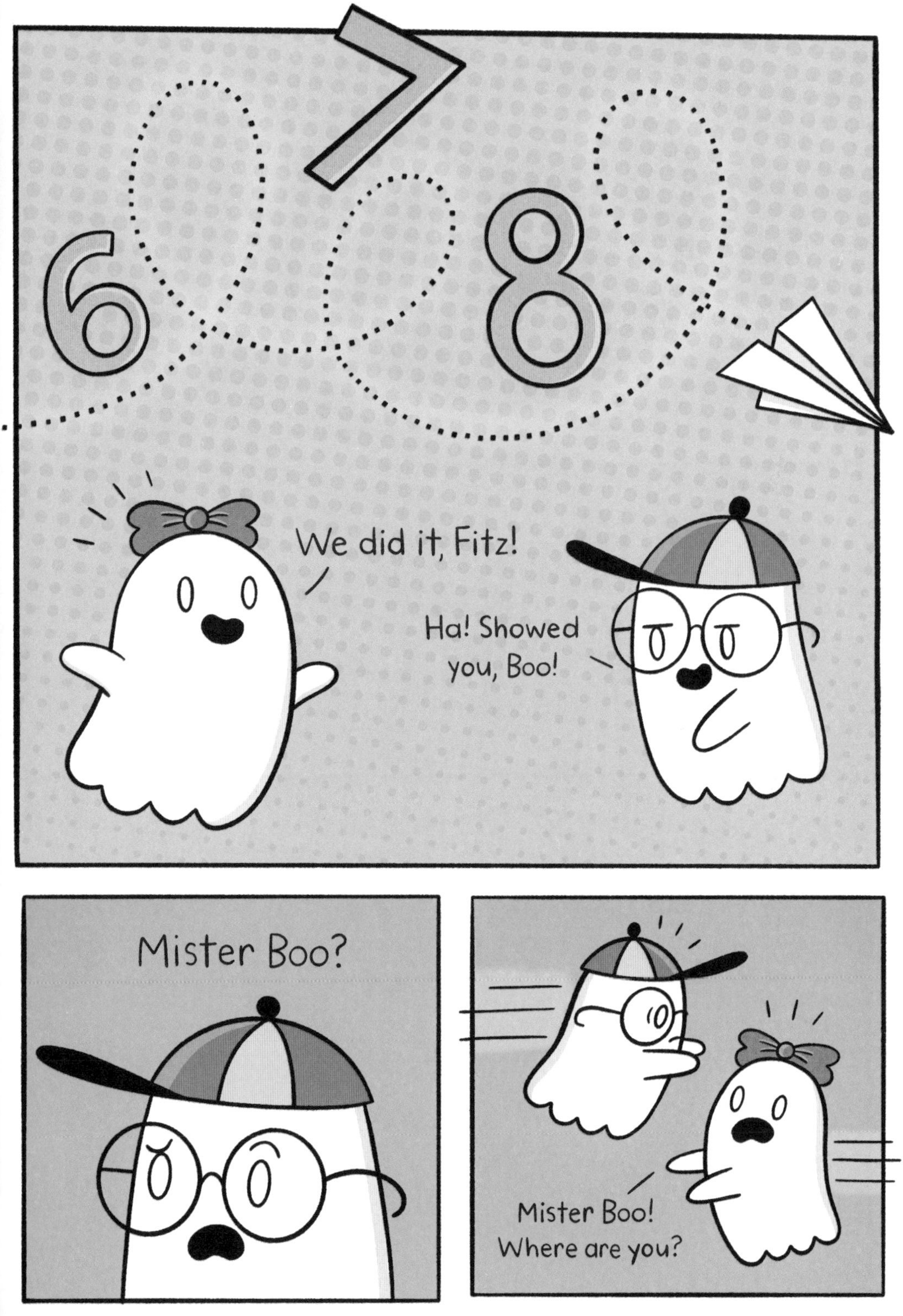
6
7
8
We did it, Fitz!
Ha! Showed you, Boo!
Mister Boo?
Mister Boo! Where are you?

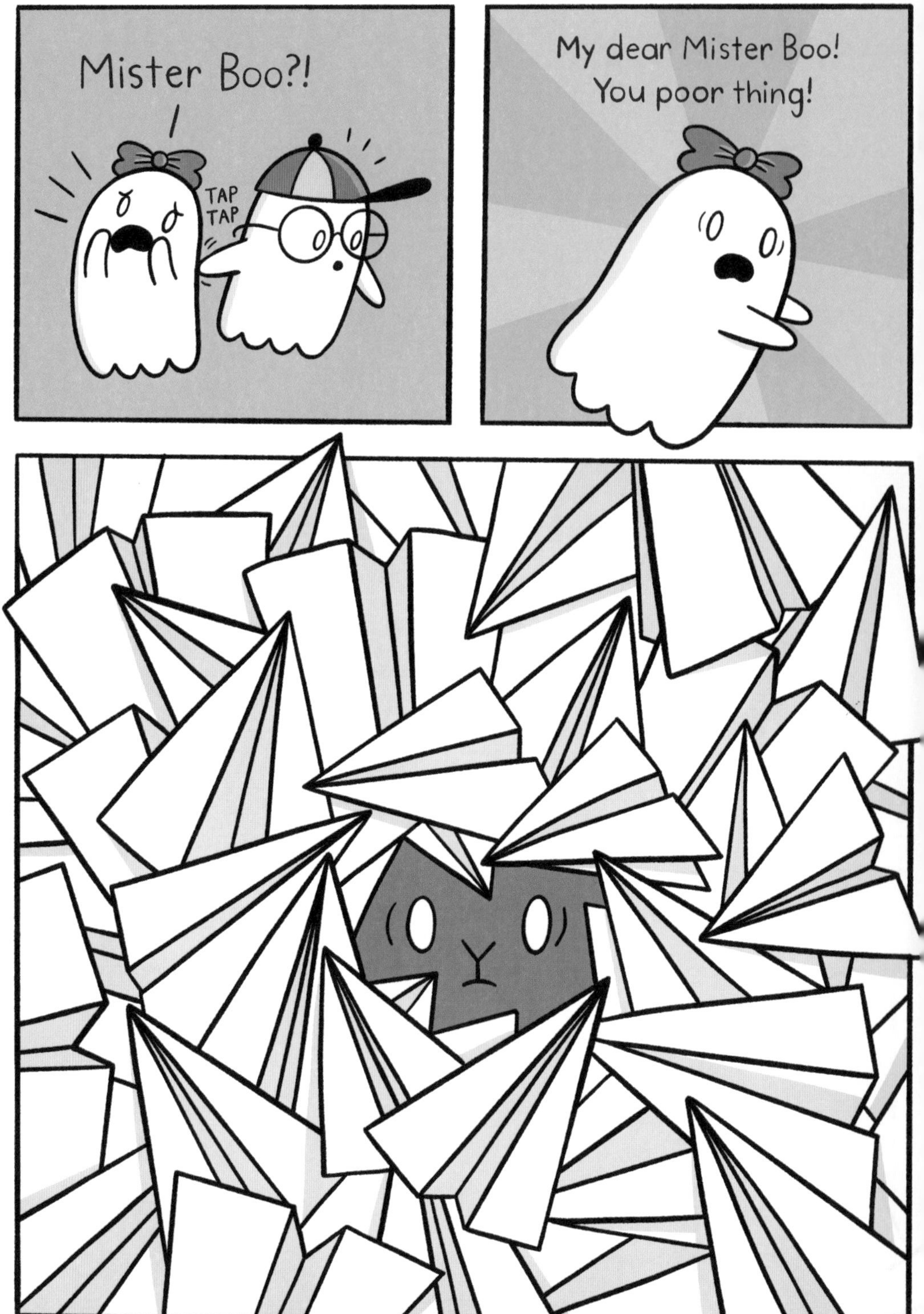
Mister Boo?!
TAP
TAP
My dear Mister Boo!
You poor thing!

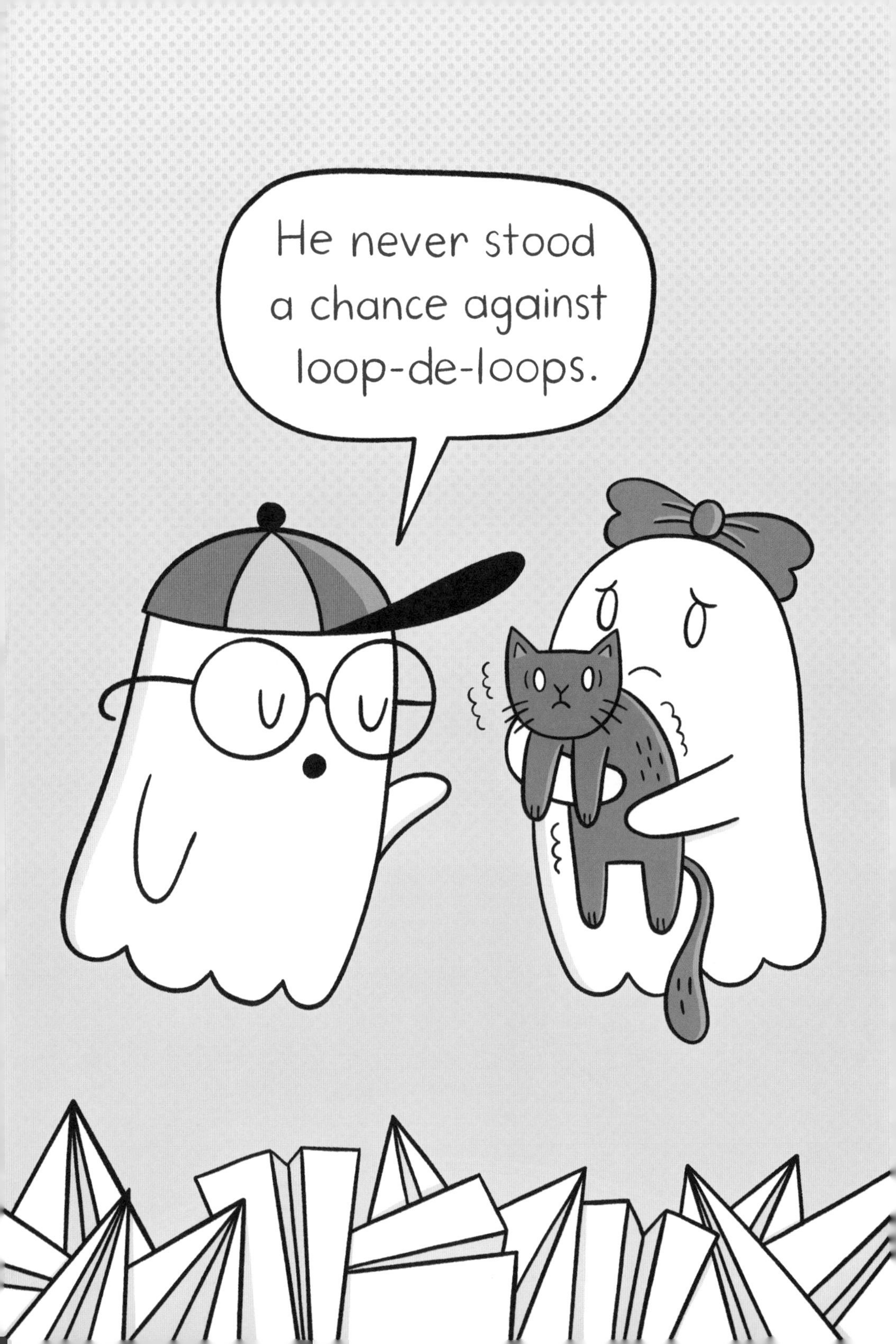
He never stood a chance against loop-de-loops.

# String Theory

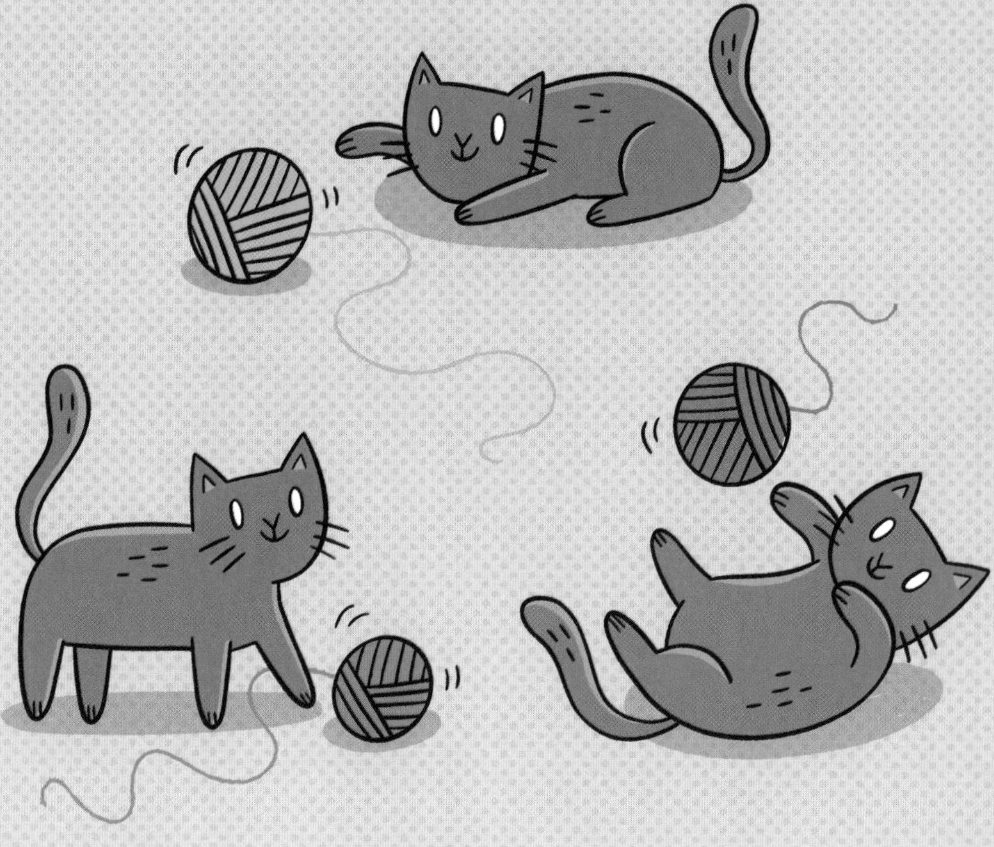

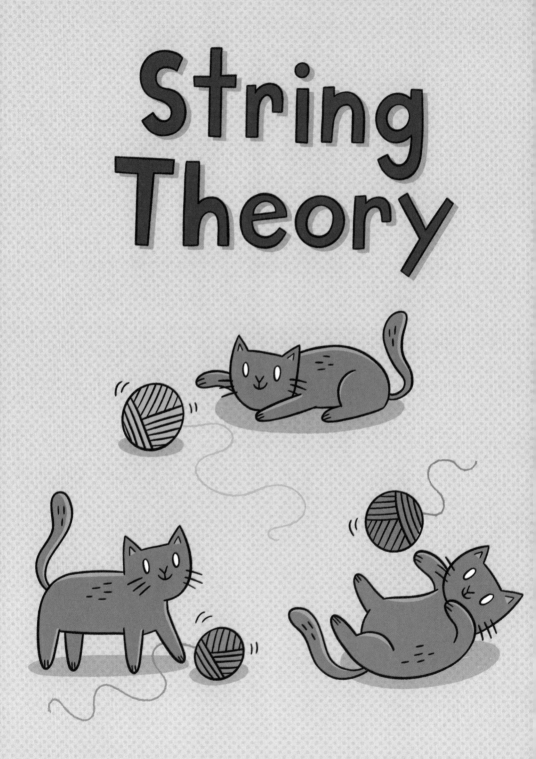

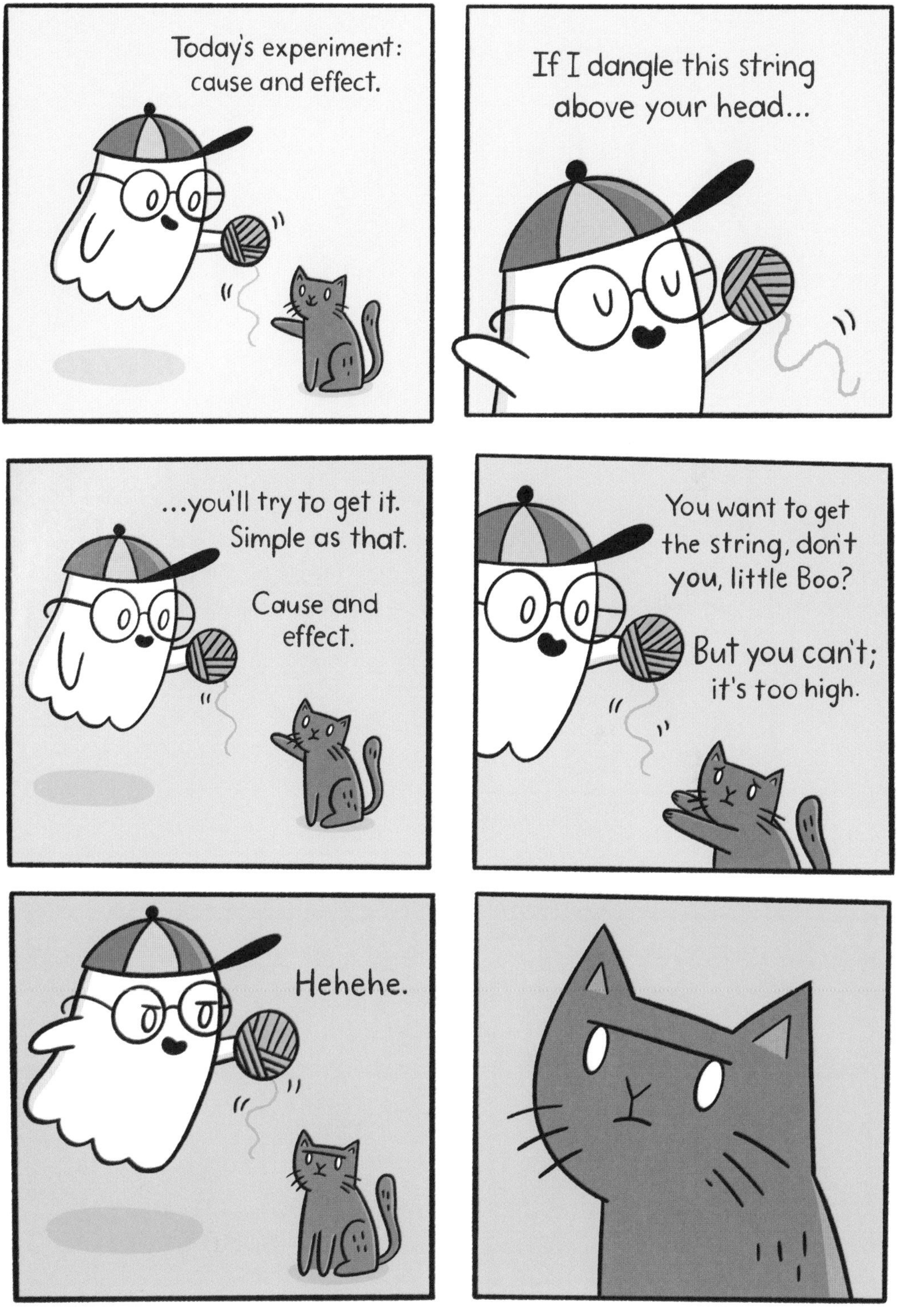
Today's experiment: cause and effect.
If I dangle this string above your head...
...you'll try to get it. Simple as that.
Cause and effect.
You want to get the string, don't you, little Boo?
But you can't; it's too high.
Hehehe.

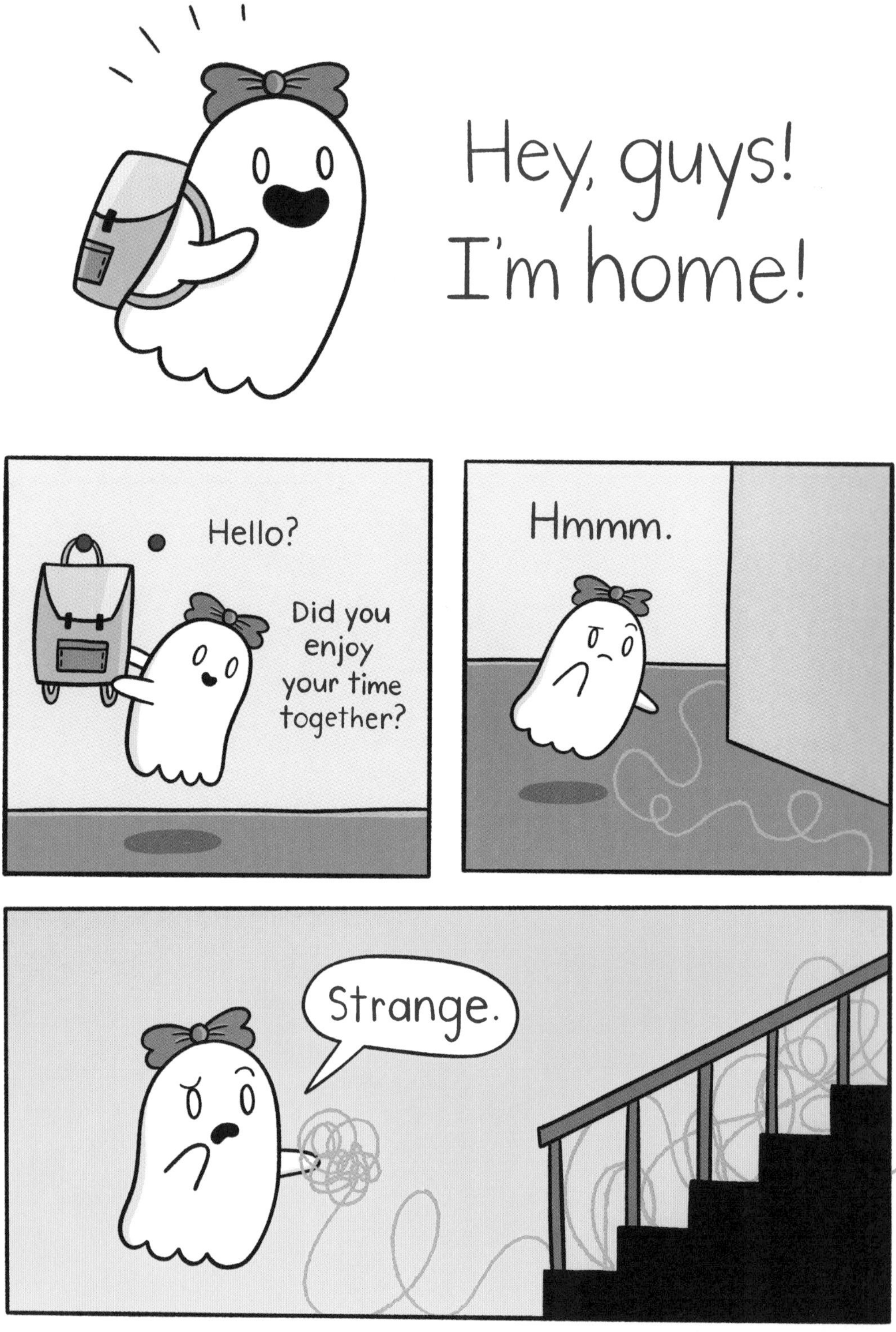
Hey, guys! I'm home!
Hello?
Did you enjoy your time together?
Hmmm.
Strange.

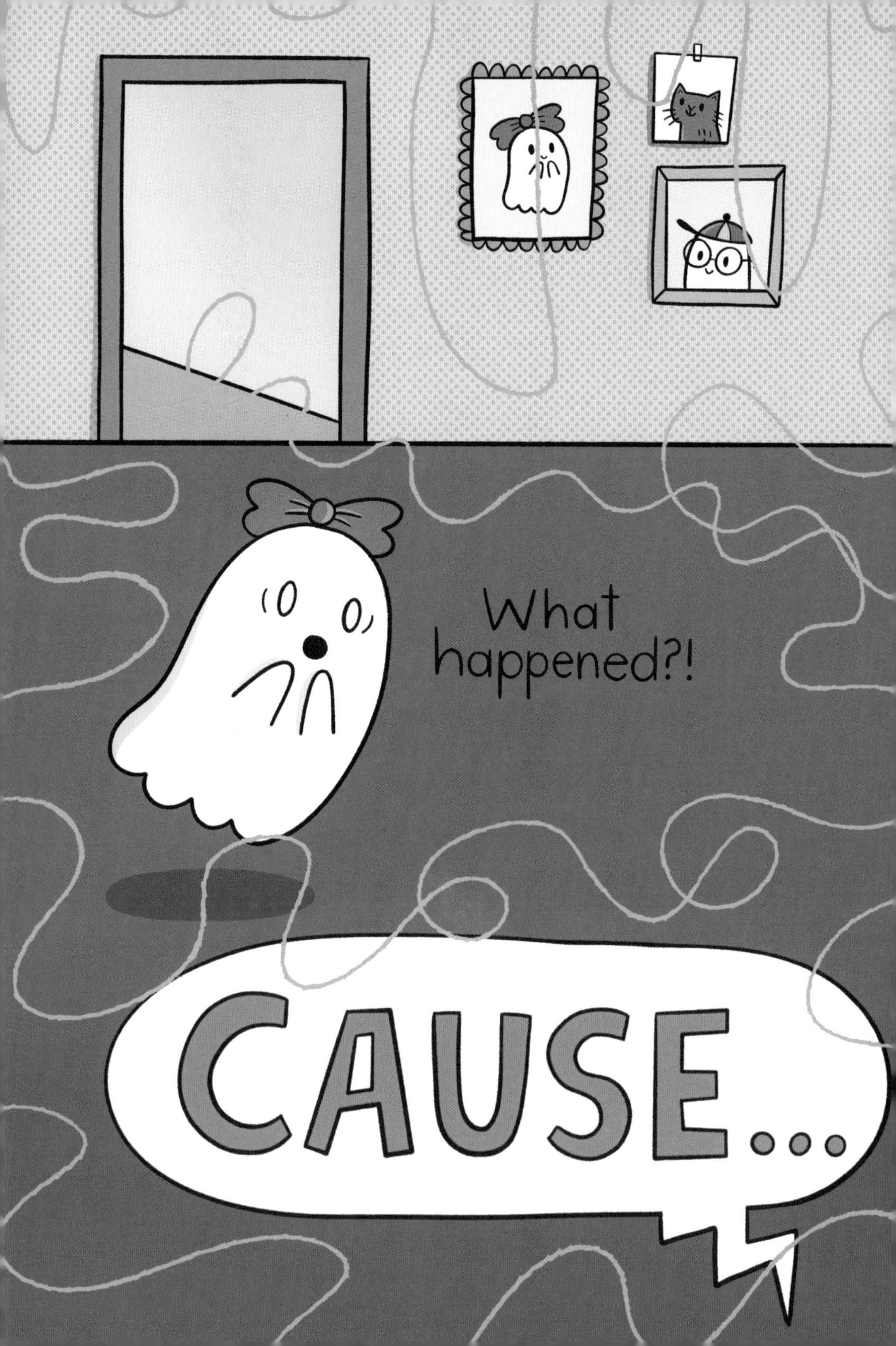
What happened?!
CAUSE...

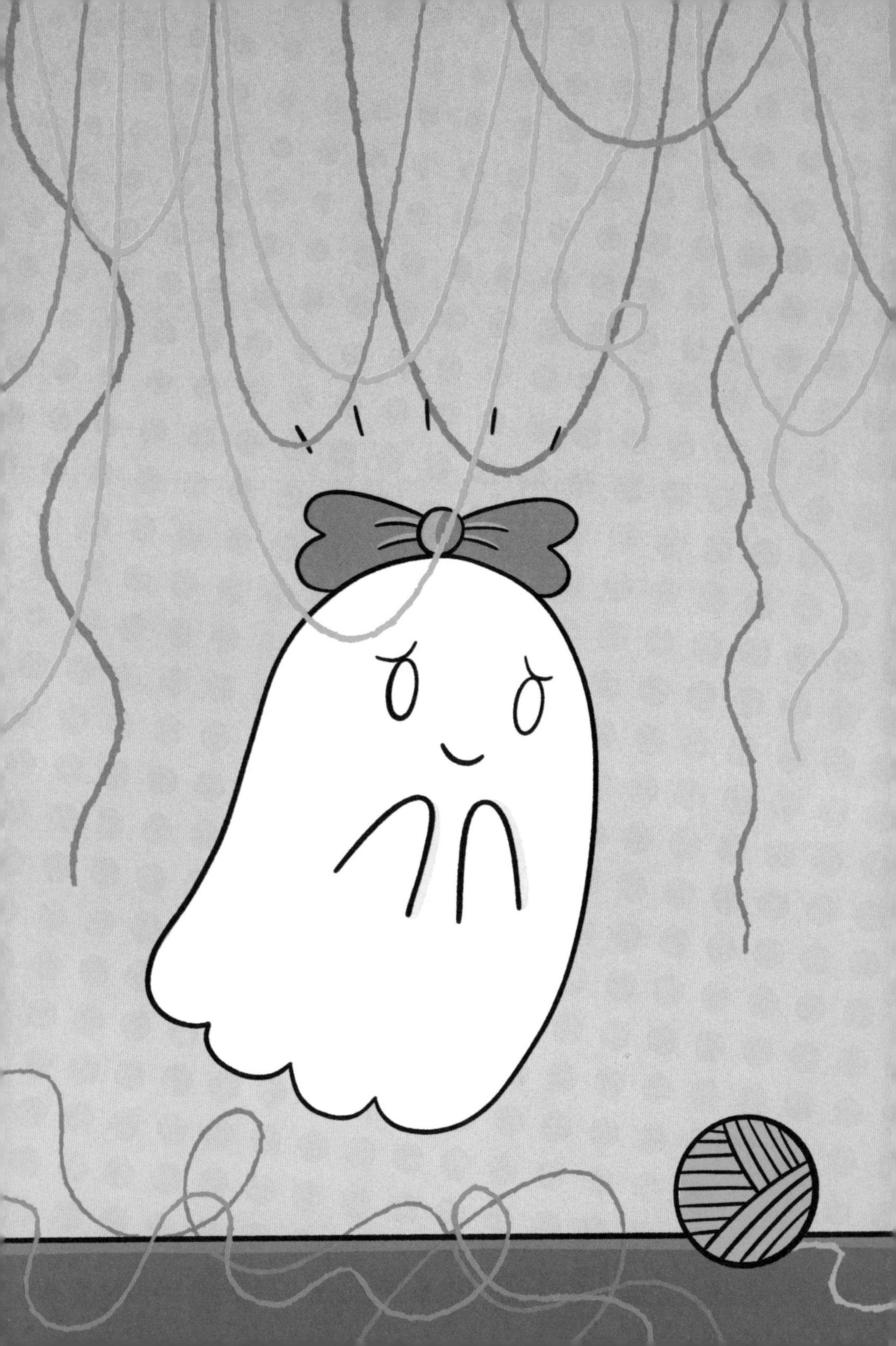

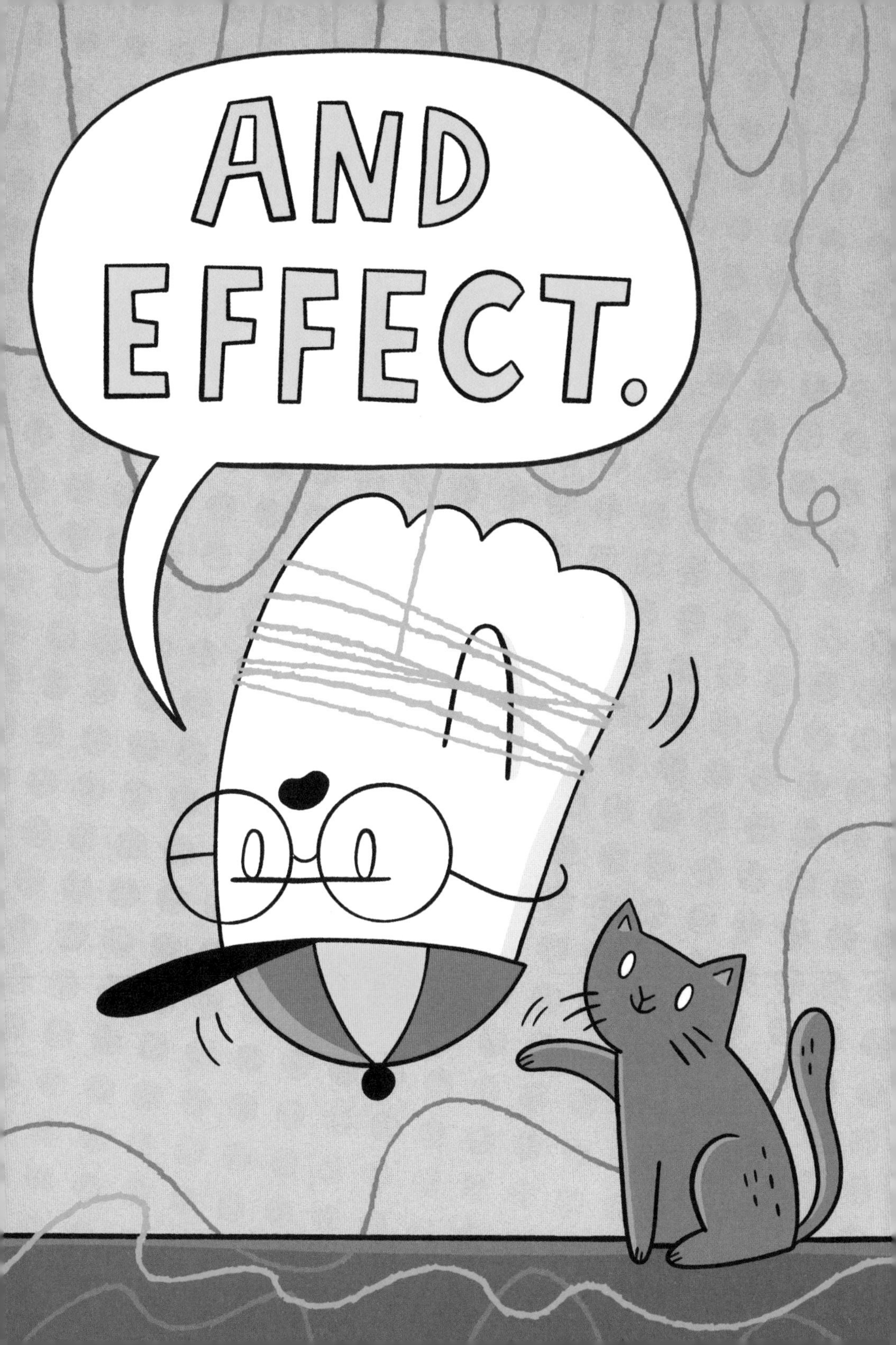
AND EFFECT.

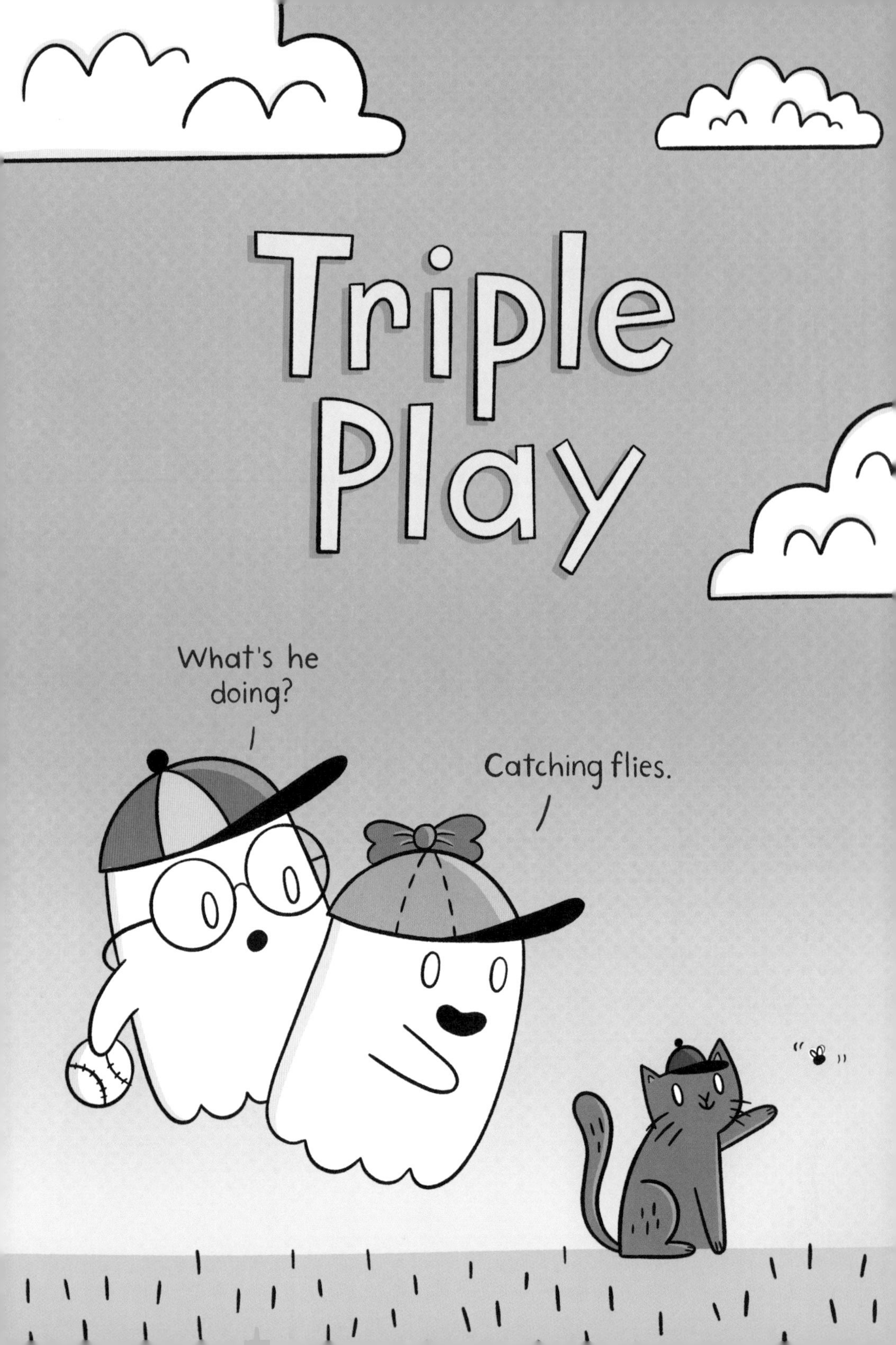
Triple Play
What's he doing?
Catching flies.

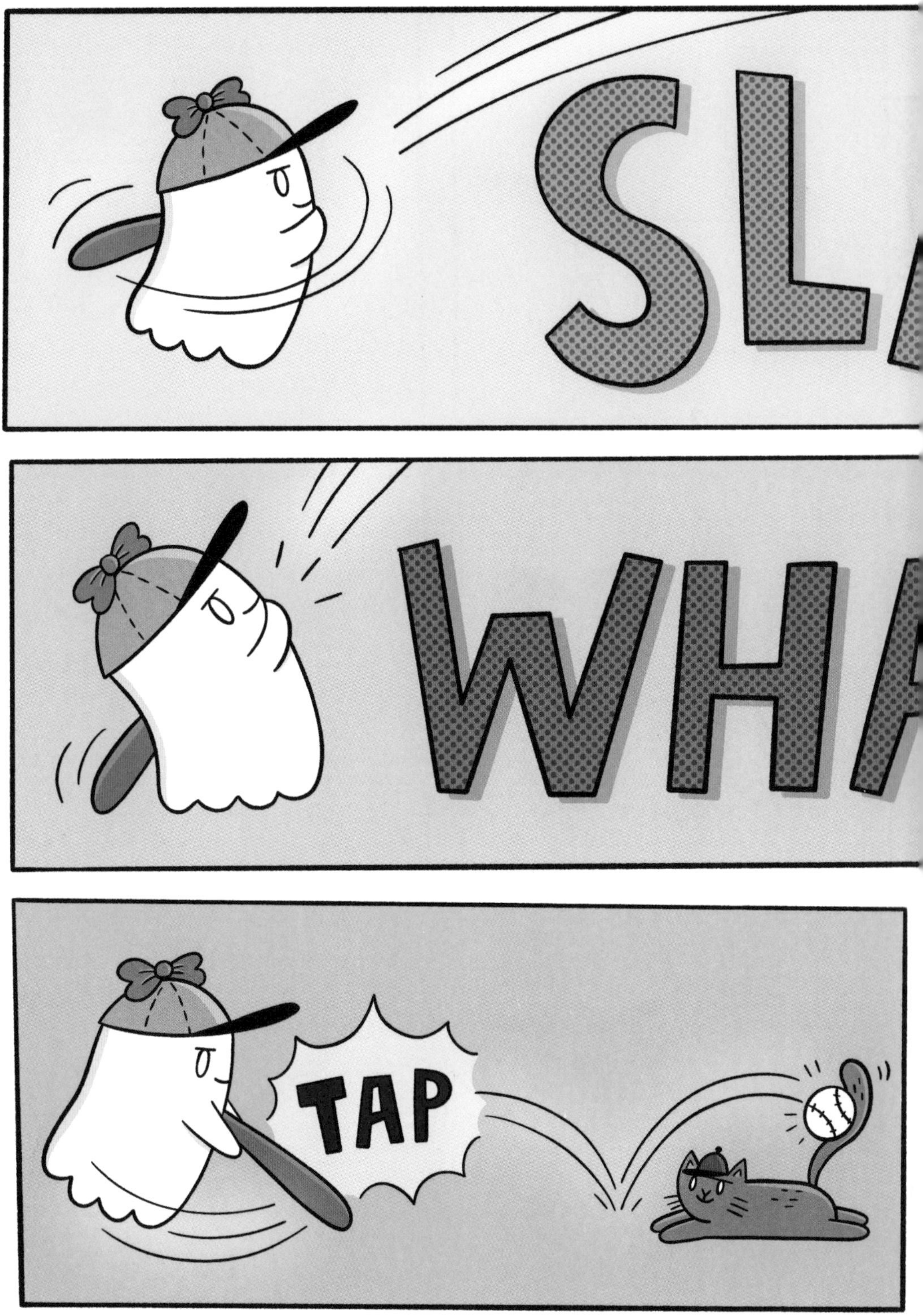
SL
WHA
TAP

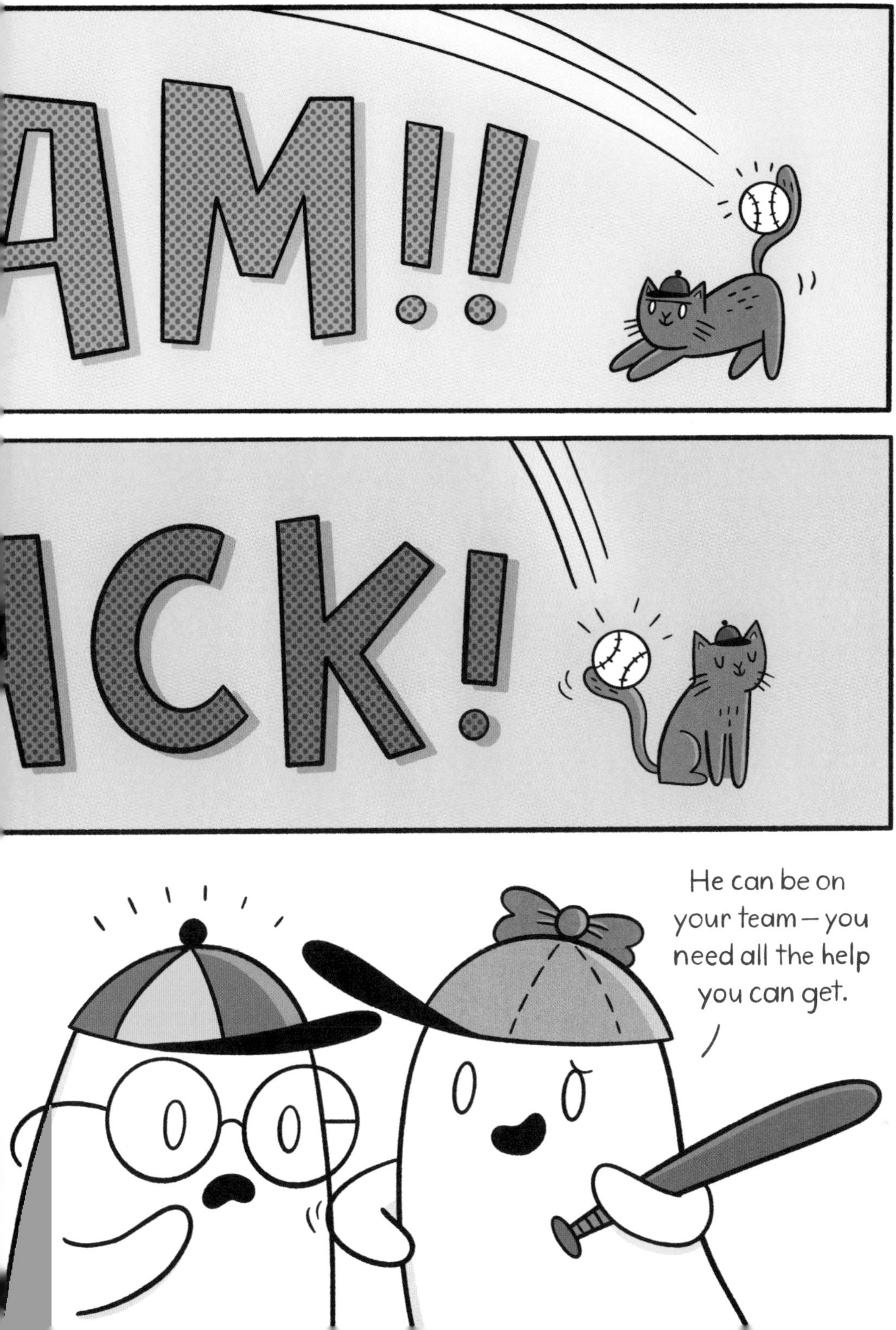
AM!!
ICK!
He can be on your team—you need all the help you can get.

# For Science

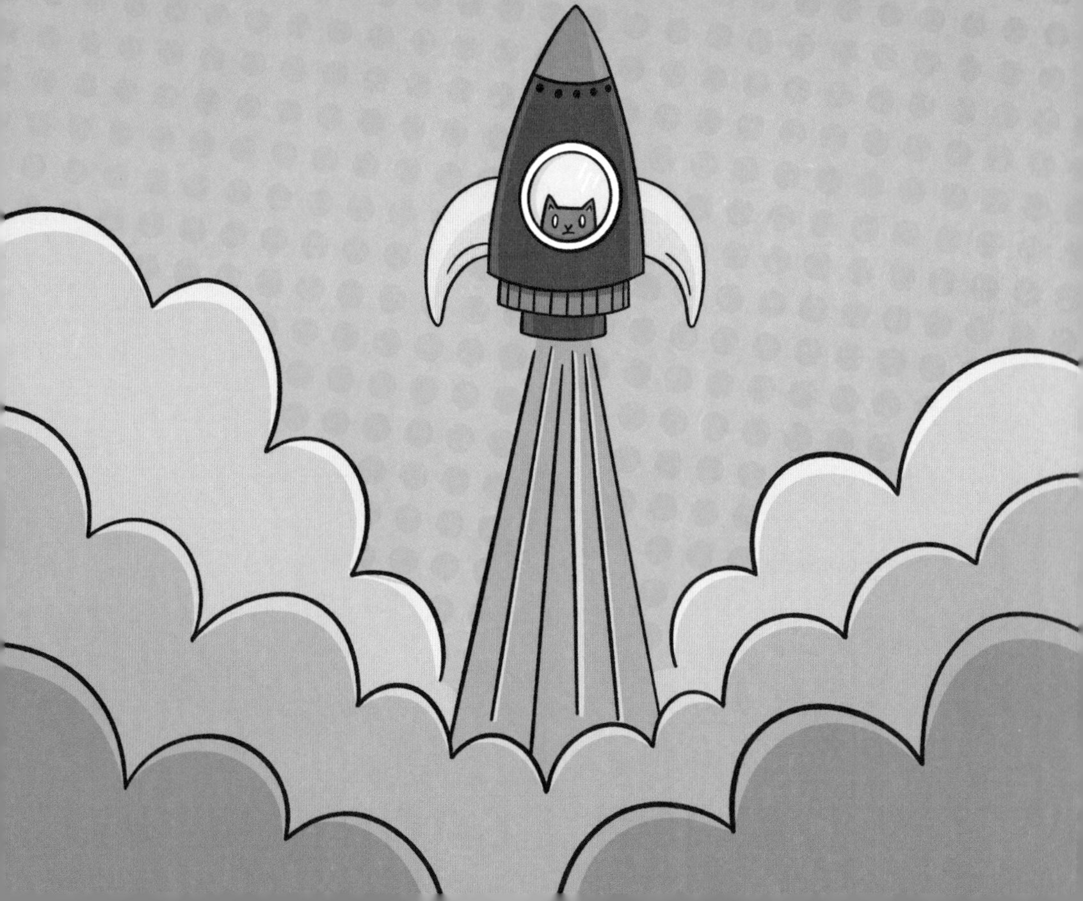

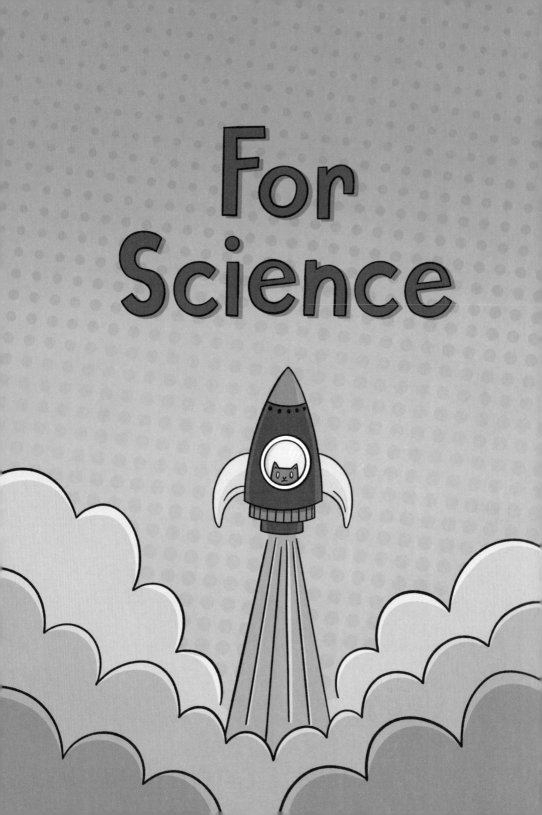

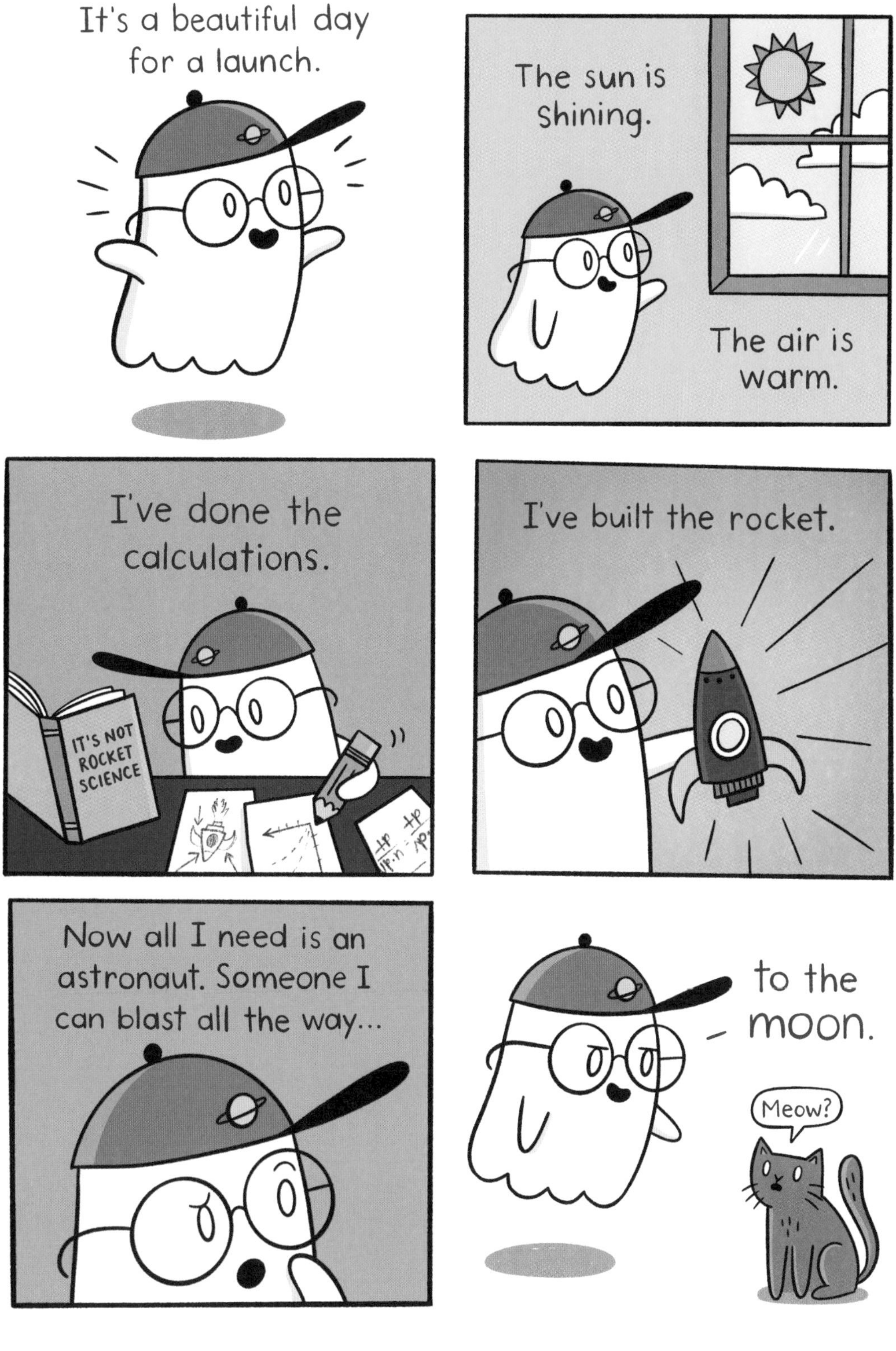
It's a beautiful day for a launch.
The sun is shining.
The air is warm.
I've done the calculations.
IT'S NOT ROCKET SCIENCE
I've built the rocket.
Now all I need is an astronaut. Someone I can blast all the way...
– to the moon.
Meow?

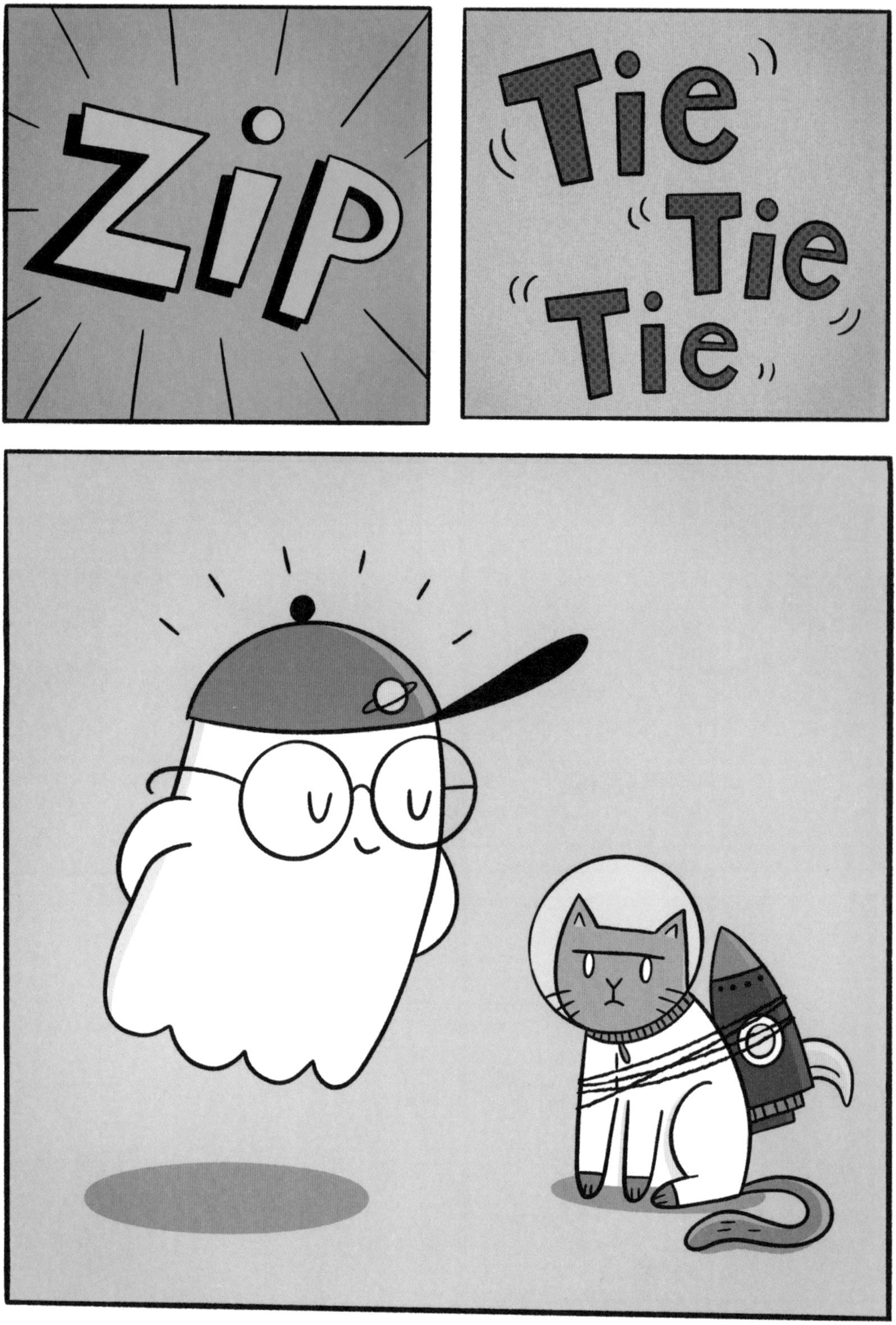
ZIP
Tie
Tie
Tie

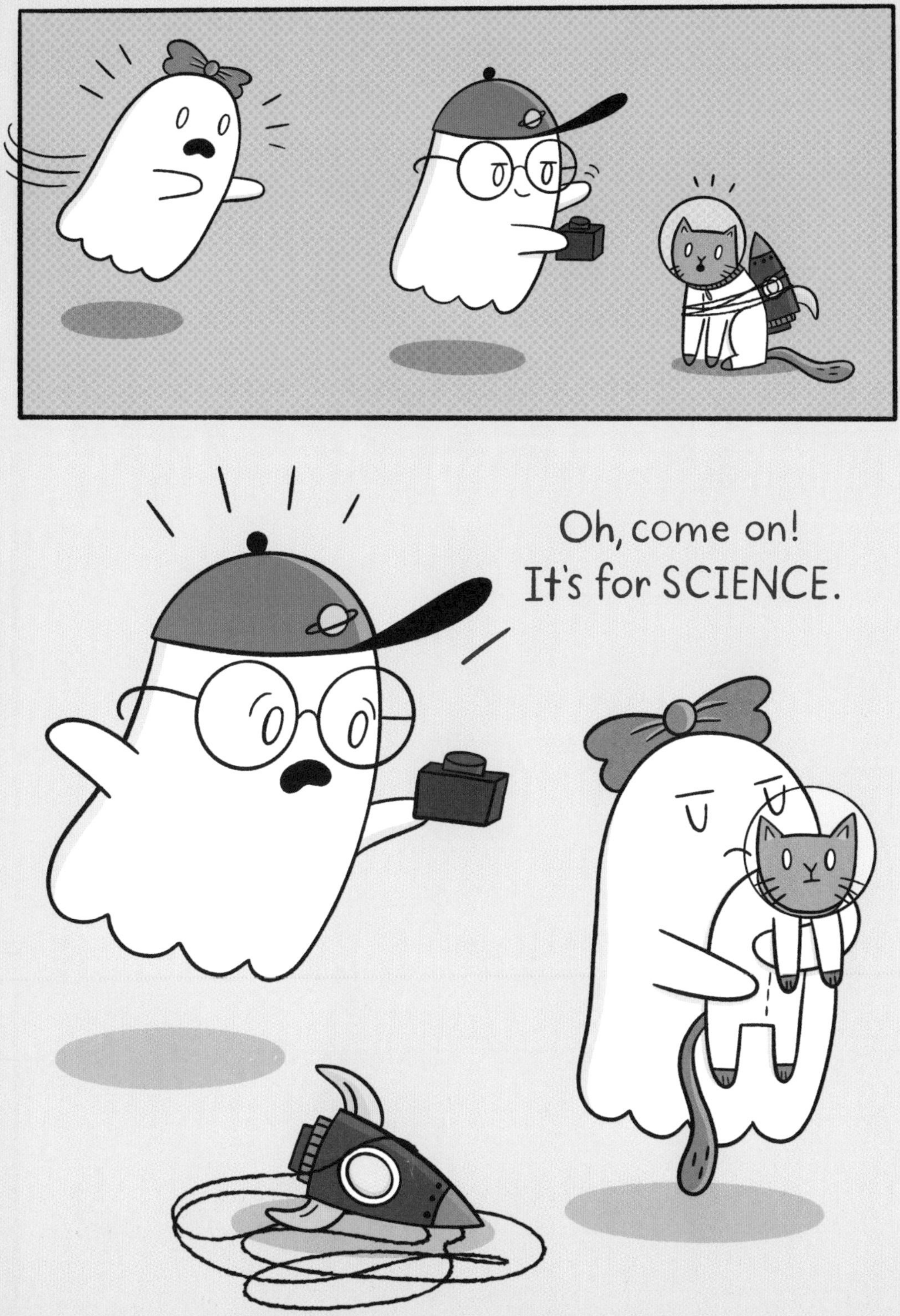
Oh, come on!
It's for SCIENCE.

# Stargazing

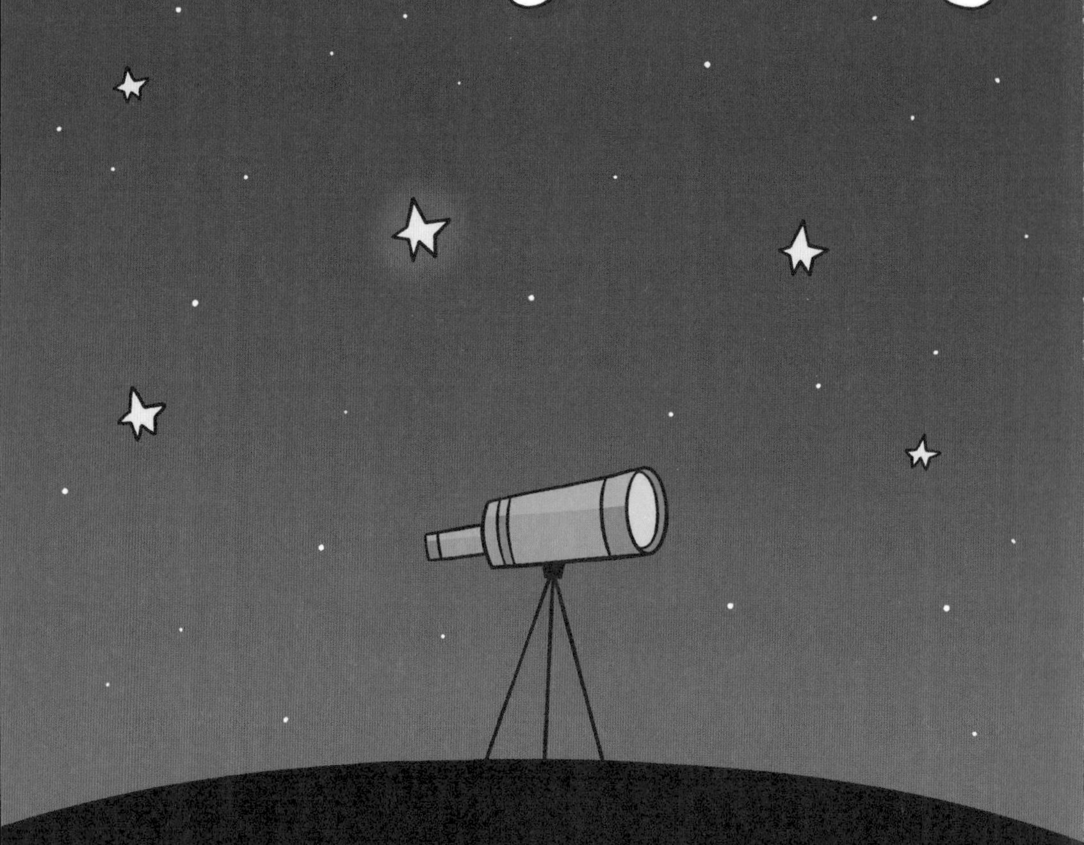

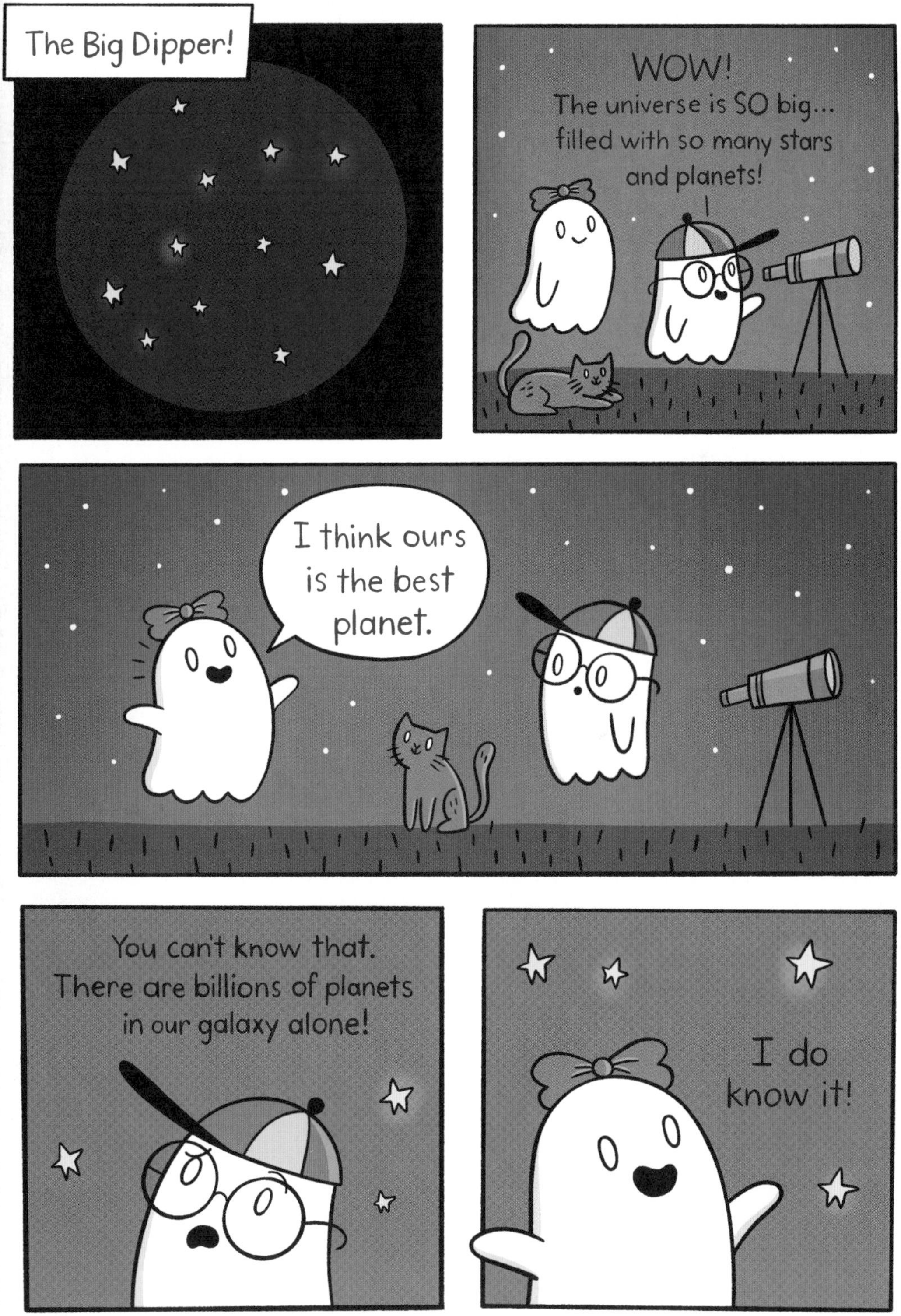
The Big Dipper!
WOW!
The universe is SO big...
filled with so many stars
and planets!
I think ours
is the best
planet.
You can't know that.
There are billions of planets
in our galaxy alone!
I do
know it!

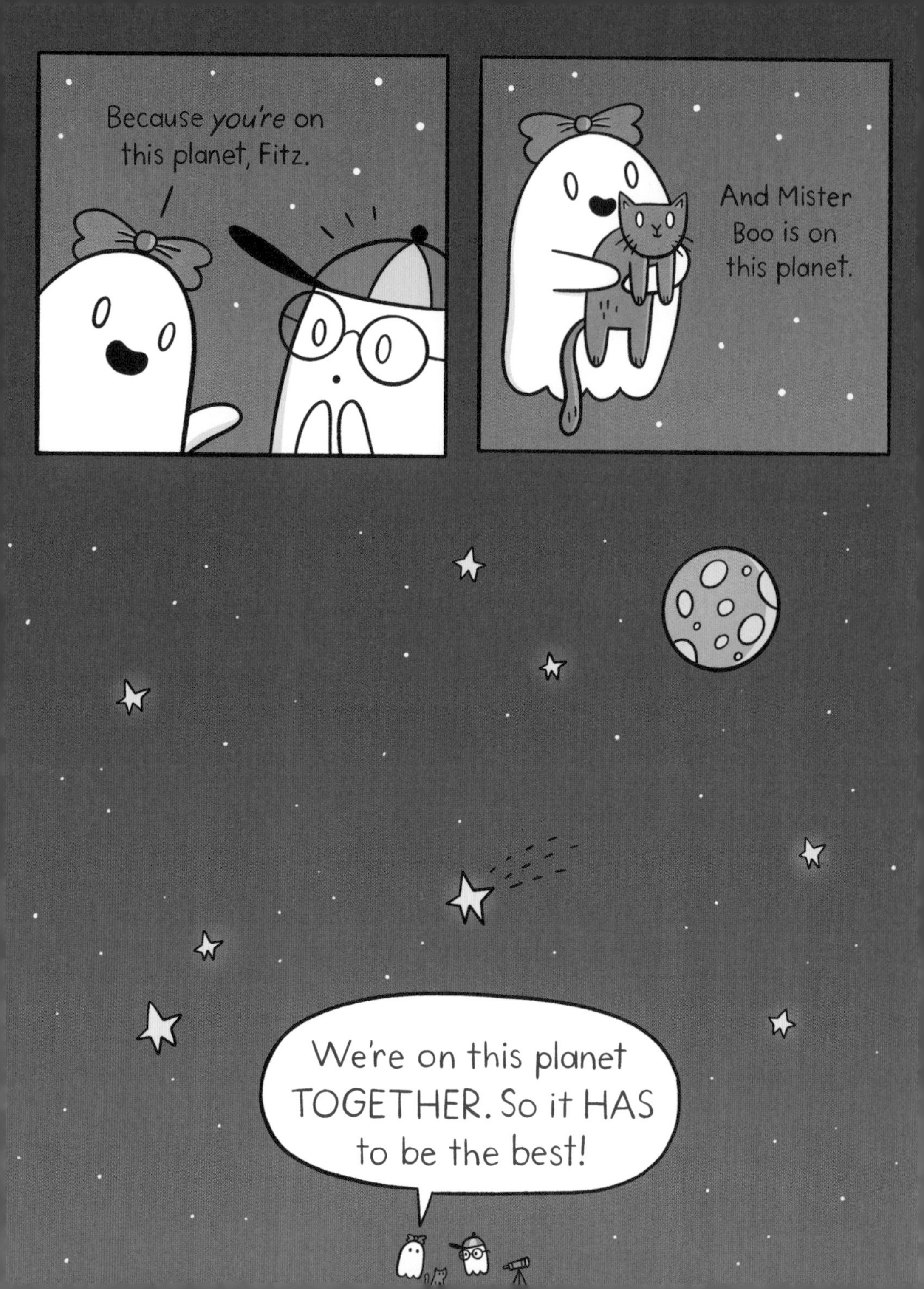
Because *you're* on this planet, Fitz.
And Mister Boo is on this planet.
We're on this planet TOGETHER. So it HAS to be the best!

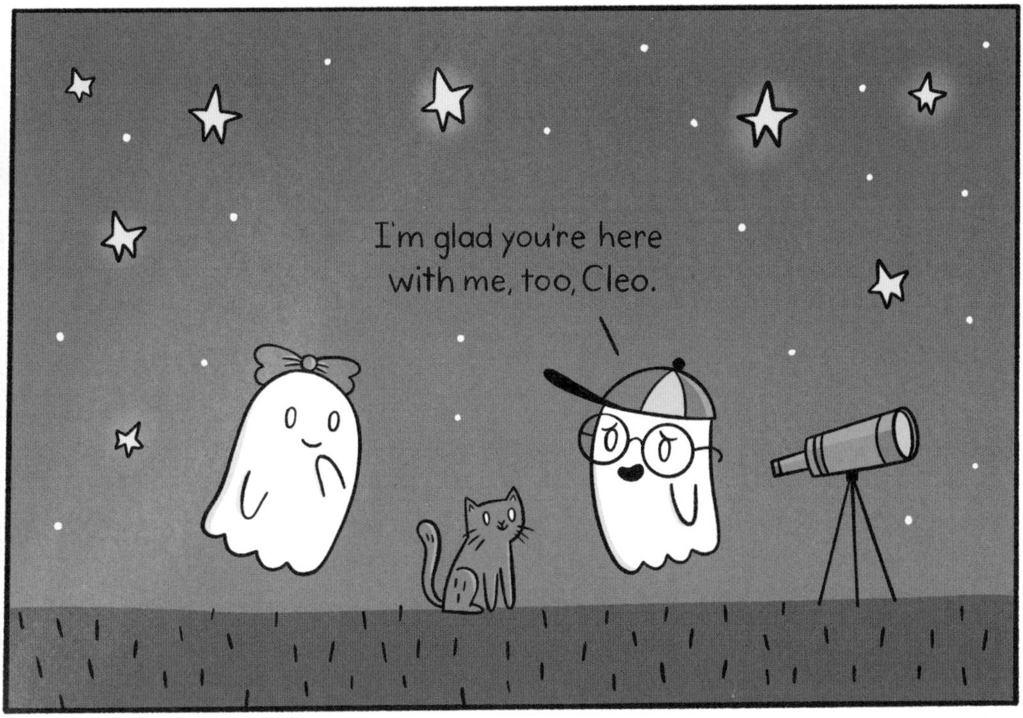
I'm glad you're here
with me, too, Cleo.

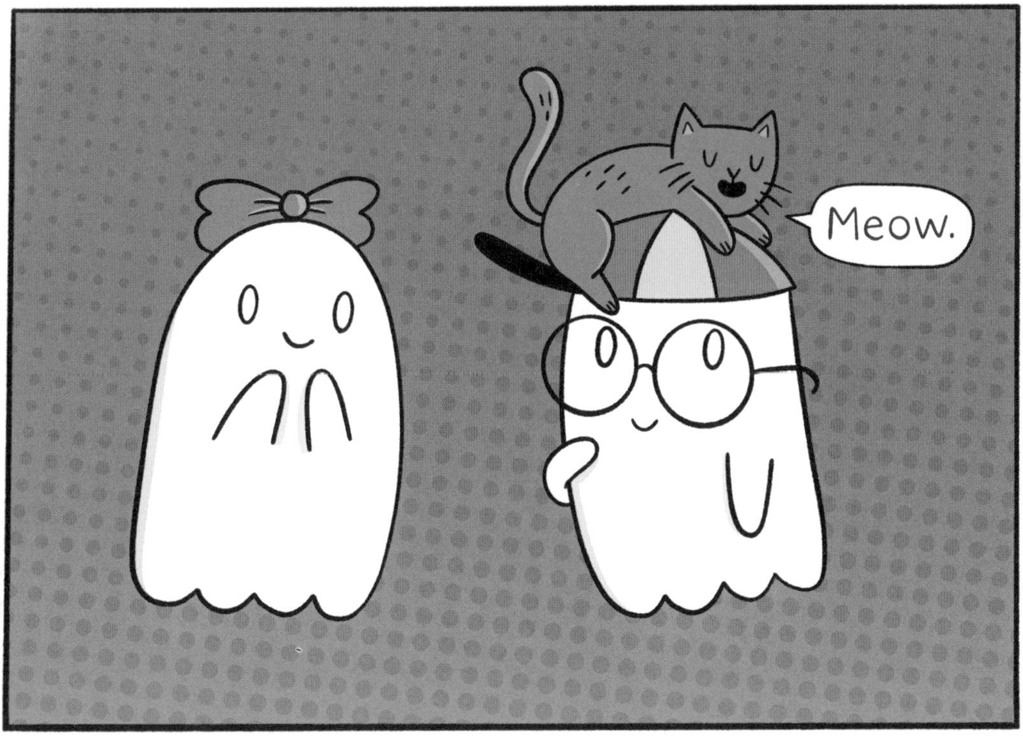
Meow.

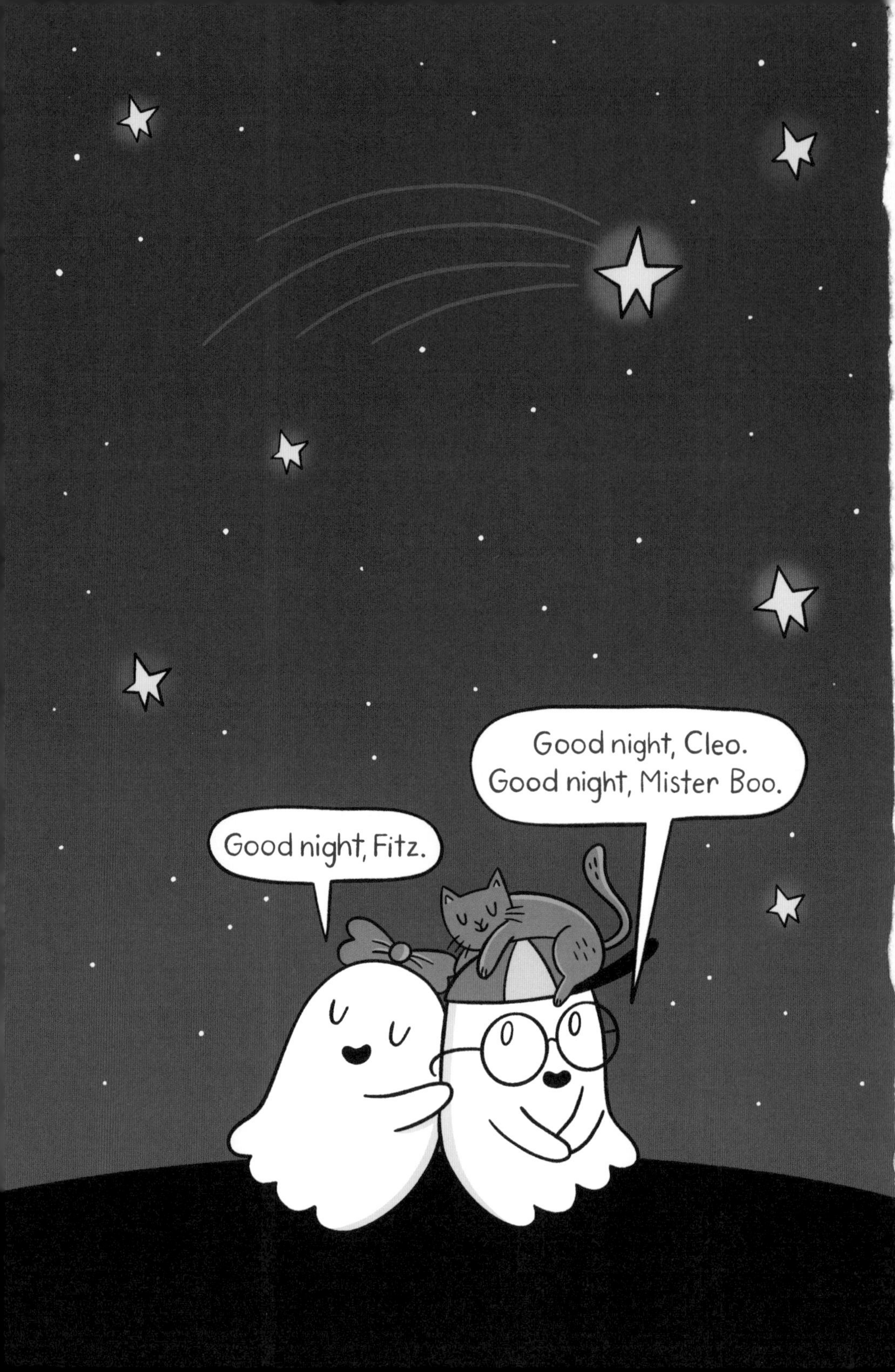
Good night, Cleo.
Good night, Mister Boo.
Good night, Fitz.

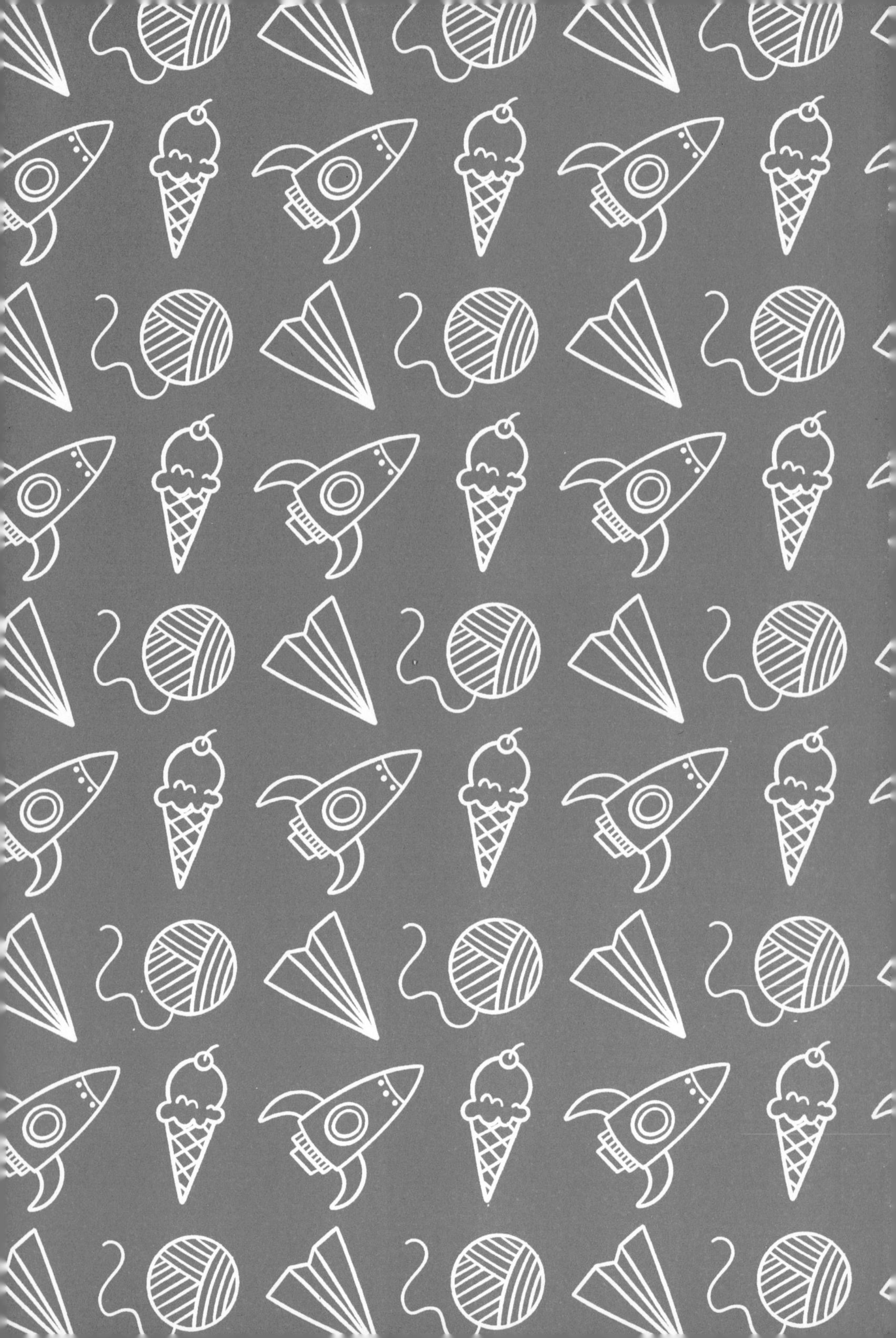